AFTER LIFE

# AFTER LIFE

*an ethnographic novel*

**TOBIAS HECHT**

*with portions based*

*on the narrations*

*of Bruna Veríssimo*

*Duke University Press   Durham and London   2006*

© 2006 Duke University Press

*Printed in the United States of*
*America on acid-free paper* ♾
*Designed by C. H. Westmoreland*
*Typeset in Scala by Tseng Information*
*Systems, Inc.*
*Misproject display font by Eduardo Recife*
*(www.misprintedtype.com)*
*Library of Congress Cataloging-in-*
*Publication Data appear on the last*
*printed page of this book.*

*Acknowledgments and illustration*
*credits follow the text of the novel.*

*for my father*

## Introduction

The origins of *After Life* date back to an afternoon in 1992 when I
sat down on a sidewalk in the Brazilian port city of Recife, next to
a homeless adolescent. Hoping to interview her for a dissertation
about street children, I explained what the interview was about and
why I was doing it and that it would just be a conversation, recorded
if she didn't mind. An uncomfortable silence followed. It was about
four-thirty, an hour before the sun would set, and the insects were
charged with life. Waiting for her to say something, I scratched at
my legs. When she was ready, Bruna Veríssimo, as she called herself,
looked up and said, "Go ahead, ask the questions. I know how to
answer."

Disconcerted, I took out the tape recorder, and she began speaking in a tone of restive ennui. Before the bells tolled five, she had
told of how she'd been raped by her stepfather at the age of eight,
run away from home, used drugs, endured violence from the police,
been held at a juvenile detention center, prostituted herself, begged,
and—for fun and free transportation—clung to the back bumpers
of racing city buses. And she explained the origin of the scars up
and down her forearms. Toward the end of the interview she mentioned that she had appeared in the newspapers, on television, and
even in a fundraising video made for a shelter. "A video about the
street children of Pernambuco,"[1] she mused, "is worth more than a
porno flick."

As it happened, in the early 1990s a lot of foreign and local journalists were writing about street children, television crews were
filming them, photographers were snapping their pictures. Meanwhile, nongovernmental and activist organizations were denouncing

abuses and offering outreach services. Brazil's National Movement of Street Children, to which Bruna belonged, was the country's most spirited social movement, and students like myself were gathering material for theses. For Bruna to be a sought-after subject for interviews it would have been enough that she happened to live in the street and was uncommonly articulate. But there was another incentive; journalists and others wanted to interview Bruna because she was a he.

Fleeing a violent home at the age of nine, a boy named José Edson arrived in the streets of Recife and quickly took to dressing as a girl, at first using the name Michele Bombom, and referring to himself—or herself—by feminine adjectives. Joining a gang of girls, she became a petty thief but, then, renouncing crime at an age when other Brazilian children might be entering third grade, turned to prostitution. By the time I first interviewed Bruna, she had been a fixture on the streets of the city center for more than nine years. We spoke on other occasions during the course of my fieldwork and became friendly but, unable to shake the uncomfortable memory of our first interview and her scorn for journalists and researchers, I kept a respectful distance.

Having concluded the fieldwork for my dissertation, I left Brazil in 1993. In the years I was away, I would call or write friends to ask about the children I had worked with and in many cases grown fond of. The news was nearly always tragic. Those that hadn't been murdered or died in traffic accidents could be found in jail or in psychiatric institutions or raging on the same street corners where I'd last seen them, closer each day to the future they most dreaded, becoming homeless adults. A few, very few, joined the ranks of Recife's domiciled underclass, moving into shacks of corrugated tin, scrap wood, and plastic and forming equally haphazard families. By the time I returned to Northeast Brazil in 1999, the generation I had studied only a fraction of a generation before had been ravaged.

It was a strange feeling to be back in Recife. In most regards, the city had changed little. But the children sleeping under the awnings and the other ones, sniffing glue from discarded plastic bottles, were all unfamiliar to me, as if the actors from a film had been displaced by a cast of imposters. It didn't cross my mind to study street children again; the subject bore an emotional weight as well as an ethical one and it seemed that, under the circumstances, lingering was for those who wanted to make a career out of the suffering of others.

As I was walking down the street one day I heard my name called out and turned to face a youth wearing jeans on flat hips, a sleeveless shirt with the ends knotted just above the navel, and plastic heels that barely fit a pair of feet so weathered they might have come walking from another era. It was Bruna. She formed something like a smile. We exchanged greetings and surprise at seeing one another again. In the days that followed an idea took shape in my mind. I went looking for her and eventually found her not far from where we had run into one another. She showed no surprise at seeing me. We began speaking, first about her mother, then about who had killed whom, her clients, the revulsion her work awakened in her, and the danger of getting into a stranger's car. On subsequent days we met to speak more. Our conversations continued from mid-1999 until the first days of the new millennium, when I left Recife once again. Then we communicated by  phone and in letters, until I returned for a visit of several months in 2002.

We recorded our conversations and used many other methods to research her life. Despite never having attended school, Bruna had learned to read and write by studying street signs and sometimes culled the garbage for newspapers, magazines, and books. I gave her two books that we discussed, Carolina Maria de Jesus's *Quarto de despejo (Child of the Dark)*,[2] the famous Brazilian memoir of a ragpicker, and a Portuguese translation of Rigoberta Menchú's autobiography. Bruna showed little interest in Menchú's book but read *Quarto de despejo* eagerly. I taught her to keep an ethnographic journal in which she wrote about her daily activities and her encounters in the street—with housewives who would give her food, fellow homeless people, women walking their dogs in the park, and

others. I also lent her a tape recorder so she could begin conduct-
ing interviews on her own, and we sought people who had known
her at different times during her life—friends from childhood, her
mother, social workers, and others—and held group interviews
with transvestite sex workers. Bruna did a number of interviews
on her own, sometimes employing questions I gave her but that
were always complemented by her own inquiries and informed by
her peculiar way of interviewing. As a child, Bruna had pierced her
veins to paint images in blood on the sidewalks. I gave her pastels,
watercolors, sequins, drafting paper, and other art supplies, and she
returned drawings that were idealized versions of herself (sometimes in the form of Afro-Brazilian goddesses), scenes of everyday
life on the streets, and more abstract representations.

Originally I had wanted to write an ethnographic biography in the
spirit of Michael Herzfeld's *Portrait of a Greek Imagination*, which
weaves its way back and forth between the consciousness of a novelist and contemporary Greek society.[3] How might Brazilian society
look, I wondered, from the perspective of someone who is often
spoken of as if she were not a member of society at all and who
doesn't speak of herself as if she were one? The anthropologist Keith
Hart has suggested that "each of us embarks on a journey outward
into the world and inward into the self. We are, as Durkheim said, at
once collective and individual. Society is mysterious to us because
we have lived in it and it now dwells inside us at a level that is not
ordinarily visible from the perspective of everyday life. Writing is
one way we try to bring the two into some mutual understanding
that we can share with others."[4]

Bruna's life, it seemed to me, offered unique vistas onto both individualism, at one extreme, and Brazilian society, at another. Her
lived experience had taken her through *favelas* and into the streets,
to reformatories and jails but also into boyhood and the life of a
transgendered prostitute; she had lived as a child, as an adult, and
as a black Brazilian.[5] As one of Recife's few surviving members of
her generation of street children, her short but frighteningly event-
ful life was one of the only sources on the scores of her peers who
never lived to become adults. Whereas it would be difficult to find a

more certain social outcast in Brazil than a dark-skinned, destitute, homosexual transvestite who practices prostitution and sleeps in the street, Bruna was deeply engaged with the social life all around her, observing Recife's police, petty merchants, and politicians (when we began this research she was sleeping outside an important government building). She socialized with everyone from ragpickers to proselytizers, middle-class housewives to shopkeepers. And yet Bruna maintained that her only friends were the stray dogs she adopted from time to time and that she would not feel comfortable sleeping in a home so long as there are children who must sleep in the street.

By 2002, my interviews with Bruna spanned an entire decade and had reached a thousand typewritten pages.[6] That was when something became disquietingly evident: though everything Bruna was telling me was plausible, a substantial amount happened to be untrue. In one of the recorded interviews she conducted in my absence, she spoke with a young prostitute named Michele who explained why she had decided to leave home and live in the street, what led her to become a prostitute, what it was like to go out with johns she didn't know, and how she spent the money. At one point in the taped exchange between Bruna and Michele, the improbably high voice of this "girl" suddenly became Bruna's. The interviewer and the interviewed were one and the same. Nothing Michele had said seemed unlikely, there was nothing that could not have been true. It was just that Michele didn't say those things, nor did she exist. Or did she? Bruna, as mentioned, had once called herself Michele Bombom. Was it Bruna interviewing a former self? Other characters and events in Bruna's life were likewise invented: a "sister" who died of the mosquito-borne illness dengue never existed, as I later learned from Bruna's mother, and a murder that had taken the life of a fellow sex worker in 1999 was in every detail the same that took the life of another sex worker in 2002. Bruna, despite always maintaining that what she most wanted in life was to leave the street, spurned real opportunities to do so. Yet she probably owed her very survival to the ability to imagine; not only did she earn her living by peddling sexual fantasies, the full weight of her reality, taken in without a lot of imagination, was enough to crush even the most resilient. Recent advances in neuroscience have taught us that perception and imagination activate the same parts of the brain, which is why, according to one account, "the brain cannot reliably distinguish between recorded experience and internal fantasy."[7]

Though I had hoped to carry out the research in a collaborative and egalitarian fashion, our interaction seemed to be guided by a series of unpredictable patron-client ties. I was the patron in the sense that I was sponsoring the research and offered a measure of economic security.[8] I received more than one phone call late at night when Bruna would say something like this: "I was just wondering if you were coming into the city, because I haven't got any money and I'm hungry. But if not, don't worry. I can just go out onto the avenue . . ." She may have also seen me as the client, someone seeking something from her and who depended on her collaboration, someone who needed her story.

My research could have been rendered an ethnography, the traditional genre of anthropologists, but in reading over the transcriptions it struck me that all of this—the records of our conversations, my fieldnotes, the constant second-guessing on both our parts, the misfortunes of invented characters who brought forth real tears in Bruna—was more suited to fiction. Rather than trying to unravel the distortions on the dozens of hours of recordings, I found that in translating and reworking half a sentence from page 7 of the transcriptions and combining it with half a sentence from page 704, I had something like the verse of a prose poem. There is a great beauty to Bruna's words, which inspired phrases here and there in parts 1 and 3 of this book and more extensively in part 2. And even where the words weren't beautiful, images appeared that clearly belonged more to the realm of literature than to the social sciences. The only way to do justice to her life, it seemed to me, was to yield to her inventions.

Creation is not the exclusive domain of God, of mothers, or of first-world writers, she seemed to say, I can do it myself. Bruna was adept at guessing the fantasies of her clients (does this one want a man with breasts or a woman with a penis?) and bringing those fantasies to life. Gender was one realm in which she had already reinvented herself, in this case as a putative woman—through dress, demeanor, the pitch of her voice, her peculiar sashay, the use of feminine adjectives in self-reference, and by assuming what Brazilians call the "passive," or receptive, role in sex.[9] She was inventing not only her gender but also her nature, as if she herself were a character in multiple and concurrent scripts. For concerned housewives who served her meals or gave her food for her dogs, Bruna was the tame object of charity: a representative of the deserving poor, a Catholic (who never mentioned her devotion to the saints of the Afro-Brazilian pantheon), someone who did not steal or drink or seem to use drugs. When I first met her in 1992 and she belonged to the National Movement of Street Children, she sometimes presented herself as a member of an excluded underclass whose lot could be improved only through political organizing. For journalists she was an exotic item, when it suited her, while for fellow street children, she was frequently an arbiter of disputes, a protective figure for the girls and the very young. For clients, one can only guess what she represented.

One afternoon Bruna and I were walking across the city center when she suddenly announced, "Bruna: slave of reality, freed by her dreams." She asked me to write it down for my book. Another day she explained that she had chosen her first name to honor Bruna Lombardi and her last name for Lúcia Veríssimo, "two Brazilian actresses I admire a lot." The poignancy of the last name—Veríssimo—is worth noting; *vero* means true in Italian (and is close enough to the Portuguese to be understood by Brazilians), while "issimo" is the superlative suffix in both languages. The name she chose for herself, in other words, means the truest, the absolute truth, the most authentic. When Bruna did things like call me at night to tell me she was hungry (perhaps just a couple of days after I had given her an amount that was to have lasted a month), it wasn't so much a question of whether she was telling lies or the truth. There was a continuum along which both of us were traveling, sometimes colliding. What Bruna was telling me was not implausible (perhaps she really had paid off her debts and was left with nothing), and it was consistent with the version of herself that she offered me: the Bruna who spoke of every trick she turned as an indignity and who knew I sought other ways for her to earn her money, the Bruna who—as she expressed to me several times—was at last finding the willpower to stop using drugs, to respect herself, to imagine a different future. It was the telling of her life story, she maintained, that had brought about that change in her, a sort of rebirth. The smell of glue lingered on her breath, but somehow the change also struck me as real, as being the absolute truth, the one born of the fiction we want to be.

At its most elemental, *After Life* is the story of an encounter between a researcher and a homeless youth. Readers may also find, however, that it is about motherhood, mental illness, gender, violence, giving, individualism, and the search for happiness, among other things. In the spirit of Bruna's testimony, the novel invents characters, distorts events, and omits information. It is not a true story, but it aims to depict a world that could be as it is told and that was discovered through anthropological research. That is why I am calling it a work of ethnographic fiction.[10] By this I mean an approach to the study and evocation of social life and the world of the mind that emerges from rigorous observation, makes use of certain conventions of ethnographic fieldwork and writing, but also employs literary devices. It is inspired by observation over the long run, based on recognizable scenarios, and treats a particular moment. It is not, however, restricted by these things; it takes liberties with reality.

    Ethnography relates the findings of fieldwork. As such, ethnographic writing is said to emerge from a process of observation of the minutiae of everyday life, of ceremonies and rituals, of economic exchange, of child rearing, of eating, of literally anything we can imagine that concerns what people do or say, consume or produce. Ethnography and fiction are not mutually exclusive categories: there are novelists who put more research into making a particular setting realistic than do some ethnographers who might use some half-understood snatches of conversation as the steppingstone to high theory.[11] Yet one need not return to Malinowski, the founder of anthropology as a scientific project, to see that for ethnography to be ethnography, it must be based on what is observed and on what one participates in. Is the ceremony attended by five men or by more than seventy? Are crops harvested once a year, twice, or is the field fallow? Posing such questions reveals the banality of the idea that there is little to distinguish ethnography from fiction.

As I conducted the research for this book it became evident that the story was not one consisting simply of events and actions; at its center are thoughts, the inner worlds of two characters. Ethnography can take one into rituals and mundane daily events, into gossip and funerals, into the worlds of work and leisure. It can go almost anywhere except, of course, into the mind of another person. Like cinema, ethnography remains outside and at most can evoke a person's thoughts, but such evocation never escapes the realm of conjecture. Film can make visible things that literature cannot. Yet try to convey mental turmoil and cinema can reveal at best its symptoms, enactment, and, consequences though not at all the interior of the shattered mind itself. Which is why in this regard Proust would have the upper hand over Ingmar Bergman: the portrayal of the mind is the province of literature. Even contemporary psychology pushes against the limits of its positivist origins.

One form of literature I had in mind (both as beacon and as admonition) when writing this book was the Latin American tradition of *testimonio*, testimonial literature. A genre conceived in the 1960s and practiced widely in the 1970s and 1980s, testimonial writing tends to be produced collaboratively between researcher and subject. It often conveys stories of injustice, torture, deprivation, and repression, its narrators hailing from segments of the population that generally lack a voice in public discourse and whose stories fill holes in history. Miguel Barnet's *Autobiography of a Runaway Slave*, for instance, the foundational text of the *novela-testimonio*, has as its protagonist Esteban Montejo, a Cuban who was born into slavery, became a runaway, and fought in Cuba's War of Independence, only to become a wage laborer.[12]

Barnet was aware of the contradiction of terms embodied in *novela-testimonio* and never made peace with the first part of this designation. Writing two decades after the publication of *Autobiography of a Runaway Slave*, he complained that "the wretched word 'novel' was very oppressive . . . What I set out to write was an ethnographic account" (*La maldita palabra novela me oprimió bastante . . . Lo que yo me proponía era un relato etnográfico*).[13] It is no wonder Barnet felt uncomfortable writing under the weight of the term "novel": *Autobiography of a Runaway Slave* was many things that seemed to preclude the possibility of its being fiction. It was biography and autobiography—with authorship attributable, according to how one reads it, to Barnet or to Montejo—and it was ethnography and history.[14] All these things were only undermined by the term "novel." The book was also, as Barnet is quoted above, *un relato etnográfico*, which I have translated as "an ethnographic account." But the word *"relato"* can be translated in two quite different ways. *Relato* means account or recounting—as in what one might offer to a court official. But it also means tale, as in the *relatos de Hoffmann*, or the tales of Hoffmann, and the term is often used as a synonym for *cuento*, or short story. The double entendre of *relato* in this extract—even if unintended by Barnet—captures what animated the writing of *After Life*. The book is an account and it is a tale, an account of a context and a tale of a researcher's brush with insanity and of a "subject's" ability to live with sanity and some version of freedom, despite seemingly impossible odds.

Barnet also suggested that his text was a sort of fresco, "reproducing and recreating—I want to emphasize the latter—those social facts that represent true milestones in the culture of a country."[15] Barnet aimed to tell history through the life of someone whose experiences were representative of events of an epochal magnitude. I was after the obverse of what captivated Barnet: the mundane things that, like Poe's purloined letter, go unnoticed precisely because of their obviousness but that may hold the key to the enigma. Bruna's life seems to embody a tension between inclusion and exclusion that all people face but that in her case appears particularly acute. She has lived with little regard for the conventional borders between manhood and womanhood, home and street, patron and client, intimacy and exposure. But Bruna is not a good representation of anything in particular except of the range of human possibilities, including the ability to endure and find meaning in a life full of what could only be inestimable psychic pain.

In the introduction to a 1984 volume entitled *Testimonio y literatura*, the literary critic René Jara wrote: "As a discursive form, testimony seems to have more in common with historiography than with literature in that it concerns facts that occurred in the past and whose authenticity can be verified."[16] This is an interesting question, the authenticity of testimonial writing, especially in light of controversies over the veracity of some of the most famous pieces of testimonial literature, in particular Nobel prize winner Rigoberta Menchú's autobiography.[17] Testimonial literature, like the word *relato*, like ethnographic fiction, embodies a contradiction. Testimony implies something factual; literature suggests it isn't true. And although presenting itself always as truth, testimonial literature also bears the instruments of literature, with the researcher or author arranging the data, cleaning up the language, making artistic choices about what to include or exclude. Testimony requires translation, if not from one language to another, then from life to text and into a version of the language and through those methods of evocation the researcher favors.

In his essay on the historical novel, Alessandro Manzoni, the nineteenth-century Italian poet, novelist, and critic, wrote that one of the main charges against historical fiction is that "fact is not clearly distinguished from invention and that, as a result, these works fail to achieve one of their principal purposes, which is to give a faithful representation of history."[18] Conceding that these charges are not unwarranted, Manzoni suggested that there are also those who would hold that clearly distinguishing fact from invention stifles the optimal blending of two substances. Or put another way, "joining together bits of copper and bits of tin does not make a bronze statue" (p. 67).

Ethnographic fiction might also be compared to historical fiction.

In historical fiction a couple that never existed can fall in love on the eve of the Russian Revolution, an event that clearly did occur. And the same inexistent couple can then find themselves in opposing camps, because one is a Bolshevik and one is a Menshevik. Historical fiction, in other words, infiltrates lives and events that exist only in the imagination of the author within the larger sweep of what is widely agreed to have occurred. All the characters portrayed need not have existed nor must all the events related actually have taken place, but they could have: they must be consequent with what we know as historical processes. Here what I hope will ring true is an ethnographic present; it is against that rendering that the fiction begins, with the insubstantiality of characters who go about their invented lives. It would be no more revealing to say that Bruna was lying when she spoke into my tape recorder than to say that Alexandre Dumas was lying when he wrote the *Count of Monte Cristo*. What matters is that both rendered their stories with a palpable awareness of what could be truth.

### Notes

1 Pernambuco is the northeastern state of which Recife is the capital and largest city.

2 Carolina Maria de Jesus, *Quarto de despejo* (Rio de Janeiro: Francisco Alves, 1962); *Child of the Dark: The Diary of Carolina Maria de Jesus* (New York: Mentor Books, 1962).

3 Michael Herzfeld, *Portrait of a Greek Imagination: An Ethnographic Biography of Andreas Nenedakis* (Chicago: University of Chicago Press, 1997).

4 Keith Hart, "Studying World Society as a Vocation," *Goldsmiths Anthropology Research Papers* No. 9 (London, 2003); also available at http://www.thememorybank.co.uk/paper/sws.

5 "*Favela*" is the Brazilian term for the informal settlements where the urban poor live, generally in shacks, and often amid much violence. In Recife, *favelas* tend to be located on reclaimed land that is subject to periodic flooding and where running water is a luxury and proper sewerage almost unheard of.

6 I interviewed her in 1992–1993, in 1995, and extensively in 1999 and in 2002, keeping notes during all these periods of fieldwork.

7 Thomas Lewis, Fari Amini, and Richard Lannon, *A General Theory of Love* (New York: Vintage, 2000), 104.

8 As Bruna and I carried out the first period of research for this book, during the second half of 1999, she was paid a salary and offered emergency payments and various sorts of assistance in kind; in exchange she met with me two or three times a week, wrote in her journal, and conducted interviews on her own. Later, during a final period of research and writing in 2002 and 2003, she was paid a salary under a grant from the H. F. Guggenheim Foundation. Her responsibilities during this latter period were similar. I was also able to sell her drawings and paintings to friends and acquaintances, remitting a sum that was to have paid for a house, though she ultimately insisted on spending the money in other ways.

9 In Brazil, men who practice only the penetrative role in sex with other men are not necessarily considered homosexuals. But taking the receptive role is said to make a man into a woman. For two points of departure on this subject, see Don Kulick, *Travesti: Sex, Gender, and Culture among Brazilian Transgendered Prostitutes* (Chicago: University of Chicago Press, 1998) and Richard G. Parker, *Bodies, Pleasures, and Passions: Sexual Culture in Contemporary Brazil* (Boston: Beacon, 1991).

10 For an overview of the concept of ethnographic fiction, see Kirin Narayan, "Ethnography and Fiction: Where Is the Border?" *Anthropology and Humanism* 24, no. 2 (1999): 134–147. Also important is the introduction to John O. Stewart, *Drinkers, Drummers, and Decent Folk: Ethnographic Narratives of Village Trinidad* (Albany: State University of New York Press, 1989). This isn't the place to launch into the debates about authenticity and invention in ethnography but the well-known point of departure is George Marcus and James Clifford, eds., *Writing Culture: The Poetics and Politics of Ethnography* (Berkeley: University of California Press, 1986).

11 A point made by Keith Hart, personal communication, 14 January 2005.

12 Esteban Montejo, *Autobiography of a Runaway Slave*, trans. Jocasta Innes, ed. Miguel Barnet (New York: Pantheon, 1968). The Spanish original is entitled *Biografía de un cimarrón* (Havana: Editorial Ciencias Sociales, 1986; 1966).

13 Miguel Barnet, "La novela testimonio: Socio-literatura," in *Testimonio y literatura*, eds. René Jara and Hernán Vidal (Minneapolis: Institute for the Study of Ideologies and Literature, 1986), 287.

14 Curiously, the "biografía" of the title in the Spanish appears as "auto-biography" in the English.

15 Barnet, "La novela testimonio," 287.

16 René Jara and Hernán Vidal, *Testimonio y literatura*, 1.

17 *I, Rigoberta Menchú* told of the horrors lived by Menchú's family in her native Guatemala—her two parents, her brother, numerous relatives and community members all being killed, sometimes after harrowing bouts of torture—and of her community's struggle against oppression (Rigoberta Menchú, *I Rigoberta Menchú: An Indian Woman in Guatemala*, trans. Ann Wright [London: Verso, 1984]). Some years after publication, however, controversy emerged concerning certain facts asserted in the book. And with that controversy has arisen the question of who is responsible for any deviations from the truth—Menchú, who spoke into the tape recorder of a stranger over the course of a single week, or Elisabeth Burgos, the Venezuelan ethnologist who oversaw the project, transcribed the tapes, and edited and organized the material. In different ways, both Burgos and Menchú have sought to distance themselves from the creation of the book. Burgos wrote in the introduction, "I soon reached the decision to give the manuscript the form of a monologue: that was how it came back to me as I reread it. I therefore decided to delete all my questions. By doing so I became what I really was: Rigoberta's listener" (xx). Menchú, on the other hand, was quoted as saying in 1997 that the text "does not belong to me, morally, politically or economically. I have respected it greatly because it played an immense role for Guatemala. . . . But I never had the right to say if the text pleased me or not, if it was faithful to the facts of my life. . . . Anyone who has doubts about the work should go to [Elisabeth] because, even legally, I do not have author's rights, royalties or any of that" (David Stoll, *Rigoberta Menchú and the Story of All Poor Guatemalans* [Boulder, Colo.: Westview, 1999], 178). The anthropologist, in other words, attempted to render herself invisible in the published text while, according to Menchú, still collecting the royalties and retaining copyright; Menchú herself, meanwhile, didn't feel she was represented in the way she wanted to be or on terms that were acceptable.

18 Alessandro Manzoni, *On the Historical Novel*, trans. Sandra Bermann (Lincoln: University of Nebraska Press, 1984), 63.

ONE

HAVING SWALLOWED three tiny capsules of Serax before boarding, she can take it all in as if it did and did not have to do with her: the plane rocking gently as one of the cargo bays is closed, the safety instructions card rising crooked from the seat pocket in front of her, the flight attendants demonstrating what to do IN THE UNLIKELY EVENT OF A CHANGE IN CABIN PRESSURE, and her own surprise at the sudden urge to leave her seat, make her way toward the aircraft door, back into the terminal, back to solid ground.

"Will this be the first time you have been to Brazil?" the man in the window seat startles her.

Zoë forms a reluctant smile and shakes her head before reaching for the onboard magazine. She wonders if anyone else can hear the thrumming in her chest. Despite that, despite the heat at her temples and throughout her intestines, the man's question returns her to the first time she set foot in the country. Although more than twenty passengers had gotten off the plane with her in Recife during the stopover on a São Paulo–bound flight, no one had accompanied her in the customs line reserved for foreigners.

Soon after collecting her bags, she was adrift a boisterous crowd of welcomers: little girls in starched blouses, men with crosses nestled in the V of a bushy neckline, ladies made up at a time of night when the infirm give in. She liked the feeling of arriving in a city where she knew no one.

She had made her way toward the yellow sign marking the exit, past the doors that wheezed open as she stepped on the black rubber pad and into a night pierced by a row of street lights just beyond the terminal.

There were two boys playing a game with stones, one moment crouching on the pavement, the next darting toward her, running.

She remembers lowering her gaze: a pair of heads that barely met her waistline. Unable to reconcile the diminutive proportions of boys with the weary eyes of men, she said nothing. One child whose taut skin barely disguised a miniature skeleton tried to wrest the suitcase from her hand, his small fingers scaly, dry. Zoë shook her head and smiled a decline that was also something like a wish for forgiveness, but the men writ small were already dragging one suitcase each. She lit a cigarette and followed them to the taxi. It had been boys like those that she had gone to write about in Brazil. A dissertation on street children.

"So you must like it," says the man, ignoring the noise in Zoë's chest. He speaks an English inflected by Portuguese and a drawl picked up somewhere south of the Mason-Dixon. It would be hard not to notice the telegenic quality to his gaze. A missionary returning to the native land, Zoë hazards.

"Yes," she murmurs.

The truth would have been more complicated. She has been only once, though she stayed for more than a year. As she sees it, Brazil is a place of too much joie de vivre and misery to be taken in by one spirit. On her previous trip, she had spent her days in different spots around the city of Recife, places where street children congregate. A believer in something called participatory research, she had tried to think of the children as protagonists in her work, defining the terms and limits of her writing. Yet in the end she found herself subject to a sort of crass exchange: she wanted to know how the children spent their days, where they slept, what circumstances had led them to live in the street, how they saw the world in which, precariously, they lived; the children, on the other hand, wanted fizzy drinks, sandwiches, old T-shirts, cigarettes, spare change. Objects and money for information. She had been warned by one of her professors that no matter where you go in the world, some people will think you are a spy. That is one of the problems with being an anthropologist. As it turned out, that wasn't really true in her case. The children spoke with ease about theft and rape, violent stepfathers, what they smoked and how the small white pills made them feel. It was Zoë who had thought of herself as the intelligence gatherer.

She would carry a handbag that typically contained a checkers board, a notebook, Band-Aids,
and a tape recorder. The checkers game was a ruse.
As she played against one boy or let the children
play among themselves, she would concentrate not
on the game but on the children's conversations:
"*Jamais comi uma rapariga tão gostosa como tua
mãe* . . . Your mother is the best lay I ever had."

"What did you say you filthy goat?"

"I said I tasted your mother."

"With that tiny thing between your legs?"

"That isn't what your mother said."

"My mother would chop you up and feed you to my stepfather for
breakfast."

"Your stepfather likes your flavor."

"Watch out or you'll wake up with a mouth full of ants."

And then they would be pushing, spitting, threatening until the
moment came when they had forgotten what all the trouble was
about or until one or the other would stumble away, kicking stones.
From time to time she would scribble a brief mnemonic phrase in
her notebook but for the most part she would not write in the presence of the children. When she did, it was generally as their backs
were turned or when they were somehow distracted.

Having heard so many stories of the children's abuse at the hands
of the police, she had been reluctant to work with the tape recorder.
Yet to her surprise, when she finally decided to put it to use, she
found the children would speak into it as if it were a toy, jostle for
control of the microphone, imitate radio hosts, interview one another, laugh at hearing the sound of their own voices played back to
them. "*Estamos aqui com o repórter* . . . We're here with the reporter
Amaro Souza da Silva, who was once a minor wandering around in
the streets and who today has a job to do, who's here to conduct an
interview about the events in the larger metropolitan area of Recife.
Tell me, Adriano, tell me something about your life."

"*Minha vida? Minha vida* . . . My life is the only thing I have. My
life, my mother, God . . . I walk alone, alone with God. I've roamed

different cities, under different skies, been beaten up by the police, by other people too. When I was little, I got beaten up a lot. Now, for someone to hit me, they have to get hit back because I won't let anyone beat up on me."

"What was it that led you to live in the street?"

"It was my father hitting my mother, so when she decided to leave, I went my own way. I left for the street, with my brother. Now he has a job and I'm still living this life. My mother went to Maceió, to her sister's house."

"What do you expect from your future?"

"*O meu sonho* . . . What I hope for . . . I hope to have a house, to help my mother, to not wake up floating facedown in the river."

Zoë had come to see herself not merely as an intelligence gatherer but also as representative of something like an extractive industry—a world of researchers, journalists, students, and do-gooders all wanting to test theories, advance hypotheses, or simply add a gloss of immediacy and human pathos to otherwise distant arguments. She had led a double existence: during the days in alleys that smelled of human waste and where squalid dogs napped fitfully, at night protected from the insects, the dirt, the smells of a decaying city. When she would return to her rented apartment each evening before sitting to write her field notes, she would take long showers.

Like a doctor steeled to the suffering of his patients, she had maintained an emotional distance from the street children, feeling more, feeling less for different ones but always with the safety that comes with thinking that she, in any case, could do little for them. You have that option when the odds are overwhelming, when you know that if you buy lunch for a girl she will be hungry again in a few hours and that while you can buy lunch for this one, you cannot do it for all of the dozen or so children sniffing glue on the corner; or suppose you could—it isn't so difficult—you still won't be doing anything to dampen the hunger of their siblings, cousins, mothers, and grandparents. There is safety in numbers, overwhelming numbers of hungry, ill, abused, abusive children, entire *favelas* inundated by the tide of a contaminated river, a rain and wind so violent that not one shack fails to leak, countless mothers unable to afford milk let alone the pills that will kill the parasites in their children's distended bellies. When this is what one sees everywhere, one can come to live, if not with indifference, at least with the reassurance of knowing that all of this is larger than the possibilities of the individual. It was that reassurance that failed Zoë one day when she saw a boy crouched at the foot of what had been the front steps of an abandoned house not two blocks from her apartment. A bewildered head of thick black hair contained his gaze.

But she could see plainly, and perhaps on that day she was looking with a different set of eyes, eyes reserved for empathy rather than study, eyes that shelter rather than scrutinize. A stray dog (the outline of ribs visible beneath thinning fur) was curled up near the boy. Everywhere there are street children, you will find street dogs.

In the collected sand, dust, and dirt of what had been a patio, the boy was drawing with a finger: the contours of a woman whose simple beauty was as fleeting as the life of a waif.

"It's a woman," he murmured in a tiny voice, as Zoë bent over to look.

"She is a beautiful woman."

"That's what I think."

"Does she have a name?"

"Iemenjá."

"I thought you weren't supposed to draw goddesses."

"You can, you just can't show their faces."

"Would you like to draw her on paper?"

"No," he said, "but I'll draw something else." Zoë removed a sheet from her notebook and gave him a pen. For a long time, the boy looked at the piece of paper in silence. Then, with distant concentration, he sketched a woman with what looked like an ancient Egyptian hairdo. She wore a dress with shoulder pads extending far beyond her body, and a sinuous cutout revealed parts of her belly. Next to the figure there appeared two amplified sketches of the dress, from the front and the back.

"I would like to wear this," Zoë said truthfully.

"I would too," the boy said, smiling.

"What's your name?"

"Beto." He looked up. His irises were many shades of brown, and his pupils reflected Zoë.

"Beto . . . Beto, I think you could be a fashion designer," she said. Then she wondered if he would know what that was.

"That's what Arruda Júnior told me."

"Who?"

"A man who makes clothing for rich people. He saw me in the street once, in the city, outside his studio. He gave me a piece of fried chicken and said I should be a designer."

The boy had small fingers. He was small in every way. Nine years old? She still found it impossible to judge the ages of the children she encountered. On the one hand, their sizes always seemed impossibly diminutive for their purported ages—children ten years old, impish, who scarcely reached her waist. On the other, their eyes would often betray a sort of world-weariness that might appear long before the first signs of puberty. She later learned that he was twelve.

At one point the boy turned to her and said, "You don't know how to speak our tongue?"

"What do you mean?"

"Don't you know how to speak our tongue?"

"Isn't that what I'm speaking?"

The boy, who had evidently never heard someone speak with an accent, looked puzzled.

"I'm speaking your tongue, only I don't speak it as well as you do," she smiled. "Where is your house?"

"Bomba de Hemetério," he said.

"That's far."

"Usually I am in the city, but I am here now."

"Why aren't you at home?" she said, regretting the words as soon as she had said them.

"Because I want to be here."

She knew he was lying, and that was enough. He didn't want to be there. He didn't want to be in the street. Zoë was certain of that.

There are different ways of falling in love, she knew. You can fall in love with a person and you can fall in love with the idea of a person. Zoë had fallen in love with the idea of a boy, of this boy: the idea of Beto as a son.

She had returned home that afternoon thinking only of him. She wondered to herself what would lead a parent to allow a child like that to live in the street.

Over the weeks that followed, she had sought him out regularly. She gave him a box of chalk so he could draw on the crumbling walls of the abandoned house. Usually, if she was persistent, she could find him. He might be a few blocks away staring at the dresses in shop windows. Other times he was watching the bathers at the beach, wandering slowly. Still other times she would find not him but his drawings. On the walls of the old house she might see the image of a woman with flowing hair standing on a street corner. Often Zoë would have food with her—milk, rolls, or sandwiches, a yoghurt or a piece of fruit. When she managed to find him, they would stroll together or she would sit down next to him and they would play checkers, or she would watch him draw. He never asked why she visited him, where she came from, why she seemed to have no place of work to go to. He was a child who observed everything but asked nothing. Quietly, as if he were trying to hear her thoughts, he took note of the way she waxed her legs only to the knees, how she rarely wore make-up, that she bought yoghurt in plastic containers as casually as if it were a loaf of day-old bread. He watched to see what would prompt her to take out her pen and scribble a note.

She once found him at the beach wearing a filthy T-shirt and it struck her that she should ask him to let her take it to her apartment and wash it. Puzzled, he said he didn't mind it being dirty.

A friend who worked with street children and knew Bomba de Hemetério had promised to go to Beto's house, to speak with the boy's parents. But the meeting never took place, and Zoë didn't pursue it. Another idea was quickening in her mind. Salvation is a form of creation. She wanted to save the boy.

For months, she thought about what it would be like if Beto were her son. There were a lot of practical details to consider. Would his parents, if they could be found, give him up for adoption, or would they rather see their child living in the street than surrender their claim to paternity? She would need a lawyer and an abundance of patience. But most of all, she thought about what it would be like for him to have a mother who loved him, a mother who had chosen him rather than acquired him through the accident of birth. She felt she could no longer hide behind the notion of her own impotence.

That, as she saw it, was why she decided to invite him to her apartment one day. He was amazed by the elevator, because he had never been inside one, and by the heated shower, because he didn't know they existed. He showered for the better part of an hour and then put on one of Zoë's T-shirts.

She had prepared lunch in the meantime. The idea of an avocado in a sandwich was strangely repellent to the boy. She had forgotten that in Brazil an avocado is a dessert if mixed with condensed milk and frozen. But he liked the fried cheese and the strawberry yoghurt. After drawing for a while, he fell asleep in a hammock on the terrace and as the afternoon sky grew darker Zoë sat there with no idea what to do, either with the boy or with the sort of love she felt for him.

The immediate problem was whether to allow him to sleep there all night or to wake him up and send him back down to the street. What would the neighbors think? she had wondered. A foreign woman alone, that was enough. A barefoot boy spending the night in her apartment was beyond the pale. Would they leave the building on the main elevator or the service elevator? Would they take her for a pedophile?

When the sun was only a sliver over the sea, she wakened him and said that she must leave for an appointment. He offered no sign of surprise that she was sending him back to the street. Later she would have him come again. On the next visit she discovered the lice in his hair. She left him alone in the kitchen as she went down to the corner pharmacy to buy some special shampoo.

"Did you know that there is no such thing as children of the street," the boy had told her that day. "No one is born to grow up in the street. We just fall here."

In the months that followed, the idea of adopting the boy was virtually the only thing she thought about. For a long time it was an obsession, a desire she never acted on. Now it seemed to her that those were the desires that mattered most, the ones we don't act on, our greatest failures not our acts but our omissions. She never contacted a lawyer or the boy's parents or took any other measures necessary to make her desire to protect the boy anything more than an expression of human warmth. She never asked the boy if he wanted to live in her flat. He never spent a night there.

One day, hoping to invite him up for a meal and to read to him from a children's book she had bought, she looked along the beach and up and down the avenue, but was unable to find him. She asked the other children. Some swore they had seen him a few streets away, though Zoë could never get them to say precisely when. Others said he'd returned to the city, still others gave the most improbable explanation of all, that he'd gone home. She looked as she moved about Olinda and Recife, and everywhere she had ever seen him she encountered the memory of the boy. She visited an institution for juvenile delinquents and asked many people in the city center. She never found him, but there was a part of her that did not want to. Desires, at a certain point, must be acted on if there is any possibility they can be realized; otherwise they merely become an indication of our failings. With Beto's whereabouts unknown, the fact was she could do nothing.

At first, over the nine years that had elapsed since leaving Recife, she had written to friends to ask about the children. Several of the girls had had babies, whom they either kept with them in the street or entrusted to a relative; others had lost them to the government orphanage. One boy had gone from stealing bicycles to stealing cars.

Some children were dead, others were in prison or in Tamarineira, the city's holding tank for the mentally ill. Never did anyone have news about Beto. With time, she ceased to inquire.

For her part, Zoë had gotten her Ph.D., found a tenure-track job, published a book that caused, if not a splash, a tenuous ripple, and resolved—as if perceiving that so much of the recent luck in her life was the fruit of an unintended act of exploitation—to never again do research with street children.

This time she is returning to Recife to write about "home" children. So many researchers and journalists chasing after the few children who actually sleep in the streets and no one writing about the vast majority who happen to live in homes, homes with empty cupboards and no refrigerators, sweltering where the floor—because not everyone fits in the lone bed—is as hard as pavement and where the rippled tin walls do nothing to block the screams from next door.

"It's a good place to visit, but it's no place to live," says the woman seated between Zoë and the man.

Zoë nods. Is the accent rural Bahia-cum-Georgia?

"Some countries have earthquakes, otha ones have floods" the woman continues. "In *Brazio* we have only criminals. Criminals in the streets, criminals in guvament . . ."

"Is your vent working?" Zoë mumbles. The air, unmoving with the scent of disinfectants, plastic, and reheated food, is stale already.

"I like *Brazio*," says the man, who must not have heard Zoë's question. "When you are born in a place, you accept it, with all its deefects, like a chil' or a parent. We've been away for more than twentuh years, in Atlanta. But when they offud me uly retirement, I was ready to be in mah home again."

The man, who on second thought may be retiring not from an evangelical church but from middle management at Coca-Cola, pauses for a moment, perhaps to see if Zoë will say anything.

She doesn't.

"Mah wife likes your country and so do I, but no one knows how to enjoy themselves like Brazilians," the man states.

He is clearly awaiting something; his wife is too. They seem to expect Zoë to hold up her end of the conversation. Instead, she opens the magazine and begins leafing through the pages until she comes to an advertisement for carry-on suitcases, a photograph of the inside of a wheeled bag with a lot of small zippered compartments. A woman's hairless fingers wrapped around the handle, bright nail polish. Zoë counts the number of times the letter *o* appears in the promotional text. The thought of the aircraft door closing only heightens the sensation somewhere between numbness and pain coursing down one arm. *Is this what a heart attack is like? One moment you are looking at an advertisement for a suitcase, the next an emptiness takes you?* Thirteen *o*'s. Zoë double-checks, to be certain. This time there are also thirteen. But when she counts backward, from the bottom of the text to the top, she finds fourteen. Does what you find depend on the direction you are moving in?

Now the plane is moving, pushing back from the gateway. The full weight of the plane, a mass of metal, circuitry, faux leather, cables, and fuel, none of which would seem to be the stuff of flight. She reaches for the container of pills and the small bottle of Evian water in her handbag and takes a capsule, one more by this time than the maximum she was told to take. The tablet has made its way down but its bitter ghost is lodged in her throat. She sips again from the plastic bottle, a few drops splattering across her lap, magnifying and distorting the weave of her pants.

Having given up on her, the man and his wife are speaking to one another in Portuguese. The husband wants to know whether she remembered to pack his night mask because he says he'll want to sleep. The image of a man's eyes behind a mask that blocks all light. Zoë closes the magazine and replaces it in the pocket in front of her and straightens the emergency instructions card. It is something that people in a runaway world do—try to establish order, exert control. The engines begin to race and then, as the plane gains speed and Miami rushes backward, beads of water jitter across the window and an overhead compartment a few rows ahead bounces open. All of this she observes from an ever-increasing distance.

**MOST OF THE PASSENGERS** mill around the unmoving luggage carousel, but a clutch of children race empty trolleys. A mother, cigarette in one hand, shouts something at them, then flicks some ashes on the floor. It is half past two in the morning. With small rapid steps, Zoë makes her way to the bathroom. The half-life of Serax is only seven hours; the flight from Miami has taken slightly longer than that.

The attendant is sitting on a stool, head slumped against the wall, lips wide, twitching. She is a mother. It is something about her loose indifferent breasts: a mother of five or six, none of whom have spelled success in the lottery that is reproduction. Weathered cheeks, sunken eyes, stiff hairs sprouting from a dark growth just above her upper lip. Zoë opens the faucet at one of the basins and brings the water to her face. The attendant stirs slightly as Zoë enters a stall, uncertain whether to kneel and try to vomit or to sit.

When the luggage belt lurches into movement, the passengers crowd closer, shift their weight from one leg to the other, and expectantly eye the black flaps through which, for a long time, nothing emerges. One of the children who had been racing the carts tries to surf the belt and the adults seem to think there is something amusing in this. When the first knot of suitcases tumbles out, one of Zoë's is among them. It is the one with her research materials — books, a tape recorder, papers. The other bag doesn't arrive with the next batch of suitcases, or with any subsequent batch. With only three other passengers still waiting and no bags having appeared for a long time, the carousel stops.

When it is Zoë's turn to speak with the man at the claims desk she watches as he writes out the information about her bag. More than writing, he seems to be drawing the runes of a lost script.

The man's eyes, on the other side of a pair of black-rimmed glasses held together at one hinge with a twisted paper clip, betray a sort of indifference that is an occupational hazard with functionaries of this sort.

Zoë sifts through her purse until she finds the stub but has forgotten the word for brown and says her bag is almost black. The man writes down "black." With an urgency that seems to make no difference, Zoë wants to correct him, but what is the word for brown?

In the taxi, the ridges of sweated vinyl press against the underside of her thighs, and when the driver's reflected gaze falls across her breasts, she turns and puts her head out the window: the city she had thought about over the years (the adumbrated truss of bridges, splashing tides, gangs of stray dogs, intersections, fishermen like suggestions in an unfinished painting) gives way to the one whose night now fingers her hair. As before, there are tall apartment buildings cheek-by-jowl with single-story houses, vacant lots, the odd copse of shacks sprouting between the high-rise condominiums. But there are fewer open spaces. The city is asleep and awake, the houses dark, the streets lighted here and there, the odd car spluttering in the other direction. At the furthest reaches of Boa Viagem, they pass a section of stores selling coffins. They are open, the stores and the coffins: wooden boxes lined up like Russian dolls, out the door and onto the sidewalk. She looks to the other side of the street but finds the same scene repeated, more coffins spilling into the street. Further on, a drunken  prostitute dances under the flickering light of a neon sign, alone except for the flight of a cat.

**WHEN THEY REACH THE AVENUE** along the sea, the surf cannot quite be heard over the slap of wet tires. It is winter in Pernambuco, which is to say that along the coastal part of the state it rains, sometimes torrentially, and it is a degree or two cooler than in summer. With nothing called autumn, nothing called spring, time is different here. A man in a white shirt and black pants picks up the chairs outside a bar, the last drinkers huddled in one corner.

At the Hotel Veleiro do Mar, the taxi driver bangs on the chained glass door of the front entrance. The sound of the ocean, the breeze off the water. For a long time there is no reply. What had appeared to be a bundle on the couch eventually stirs, sits up. The young man rubs his knuckles across his eyes. His toes clumsy with sleep, he explores the floor with his toes until he finds a pair of sandals. He lumbers toward the door but on the way he stops and changes direction. At the desk in the middle of the lobby he picks up a set of keys. When he finally has the door open, the young man smiles and wipes his eyes once more but he doesn't ask if she has a reservation. At this time of year the hotel is never full.

"Would you like a room with a sea view?"

A calendar beside the desk is opened to a month and year long past. He offers her a glass of water. As he draws it from the inverted blue jug a pocket of air babbles to the surface and Zoë wonders what possessed her to return.

At first she is too tired to remove her clothing and only sits on the bed but then she is too uncomfortable to remain dressed. Naked, she stands and watches her black silhouette on the wall. In her other self, she is much taller, her arms gaunt sticks that reach down the angular sides of her body. The silhouette grows shorter, hips emerge from the lines and, within the shadow of her body, a brown switch. She reaches for it, her body becoming its silhouette. For a moment, quiet takes the room, filling the emptiness left by the off-kilter drone of the air-conditioner. She opens the window and the sea air blows against her, around her, hisses out through the crack beneath the door. Some papers she had placed on the bedside table fly across the floor. She had almost forgotten, the trade winds of Northeast Brazil. Across the avenue, a group of men sit around an upturned crate, drinking their way through a game of dominoes.

In my mind, she thinks, I am still on the plane, it is last night, it is your last night. My face to the window, my hands cupped around my eyes, but only a night black like your hair, black like myself wrapped in your hair, the scent of your hair, lost. There is nothing to see but a void, a void like the one that takes up where your absence begins, mother, mama, mammary.

**SHE AWAKENS** with a jarring sensitivity to sound, in the pit of her stomach an emptiness that isn't hunger. For some time, she lies there with her limbs drawn in, scanning the texture of the ceiling. She begins to count the spots. Yet she has no idea what constitutes a spot; some are very distinct, others faint. Inexplicably, a few seem to appear and disappear. She begins to count. The first time her tally reaches thirty-six. She counts again, stopping at thirty-four. The next time she identifies thirty-nine. She counts again, and again, and finally decides she was right the first time. Thirty-six. Her age, it occurs to her, satisfied with a kind of symmetry.

And for a woman of thirty-six, she is remarkably unencumbered. Without a husband, children, a mortgage, she can live light. But her sense of lightness is not what it used to be. For reasons she could not understand, or forgive, her mother had not told her she had cancer. Pain in one hip, yes, but that was arthritis; the weight loss, cause for celebration. Sometimes Zoë had noticed her dozing off at odd hours in the afternoon, even in mid-conversation, a new habit her mother attributed to what she called the overarching curse of longevity.

The phone call had come not late at night, when bad news is supposed to arrive, but just after two in the afternoon, during her office hours. Several students were sitting on the floor outside her door, waiting to speak with her. One was inside, challenging his grade from last term. In resentful silence, the student picked at his cuticles while from the other end of the line a social worker at Columbia Presbyterian spoke.

When Zoë pulled back the curtain around the hospital bed, her mother looked smaller and gave an overall impression of helplessness and fragility that in contrast to the way many people describe the cycle of life was not the helplessness and fragility of a child. A tube ran to her withered wrists, another released oxygen at the nostrils.

Not long after returning from Salonika, the city of her mother's birth and in whose harbor Zoë scattered an astonishingly small box of ashes, she began to feel a pain so intense that during her periods she could scarcely get out of bed. At first she stayed there, in bed, experimenting with a combination of hot water bottles, extra-strength Tylenol, Irish whisky, and deep breathing. Her doctor prescribed stronger painkillers but it was her gynecologist who discovered the large tumor lodged in her uterine wall, a mass of sinewy flesh the size of a grapefruit that ultimately had to be removed through a painful surgery. Benign, fortunately. But there were complications. The only way to stop the bleeding was to remove the organ the tumor had adhered to. The horizontal scar across her abdomen looked like that of any woman who had given birth by caesarian, only she had delivered not a child but her own womb.

Since those two events, her mother's death and her own illness, she has experienced a combination of longing, anger, vulnerability, regret, exhaustion, and the occasional urge to take a preemptive strike at her own mortality. At times, she has the sense of there being inside her yet another tumor, different from the one that took her mother's life or the one that had been growing on the periphery of her own motherhood. This time it is a tumor that only she can detect, one that is branching out through invisible channels, oppressing her lungs, clouding her vision, threatening to suffocate her. At others, it is a thick dark liquid swaddling her chest, inching toward her neck. At still others, it is a chemical tincture overtaking the synapses of her brain. In the darkness of sleep, she grabs for something to hold onto, anything that will help her pull herself free. But there is only air and liquid. In the mornings she wakens earlier than normal, startled from vivid dreams she is nonetheless unable to recall.

The only child of a long-widowed woman, Zoë is no longer the descendent of a living soul. At the same time, although she had never wanted to have a child, the remote possibility of bringing one into the world had been the very uncertainty that seemed to guarantee that the future was something uncertain, to be discovered.

**A SIGHT CAN BE TAKEN** in from a distance, the gaze travels, but a smell must penetrate to be felt. Here, in this city that is all about her, the smells—sour fruit, human waste, fermentation, stagnant canals—enter as certainly as the Dutch once penetrated the coastal trading posts, swept the towns and plantations, routed the Portuguese.

Early evening traffic chokes the streets. Those with fair skin are edgy at the wheel, while the rest (darker, shorter, slighter) negotiate chuck-holed sidewalks, crowd at bus stops, ride bicycles with naked spindles for pedals. As she waits to cross the street, a taxi sloshes through a puddle, wetting her feet. A woman nearer the curb whose skirt is now speckled brown curses the driver, a boy laughs, two other boys pay no mind because their only interest is to see who can spit farther. Ten fingers of a young couple are intertwined. And so she walks, skirting the fleshy moist brush with strangers, the litter-filled holes, the iridescence of motor oil atop brackish puddles and, reaching the end of the block, turns down a half-paved side street. There is a pressure in her intestines, the taste of metal in her mouth. Through upturned eyes she can distinguish a woman leaning out a second-story window, shaking something, a mat, a carpet, a tablecloth, dust flitting circles under the streetlamp.

Not halfway down the block, she comes face to face with another domestic scene: a mother and son carting their livelihood. They are culling the garbage outside walls festooned with broken bottles, pushing a cart full with scraps of food, cardboard, and glass. The food is piled in a bucket, the boxes and bottles mixed in the belly of the cart. The boy looks at her cap-a-pie: *"Oi, gringa. Tem monei?"* He is rubbing his belly with one hand, extending the other plaintively. Yet the expression on his face is not plaintive. It is haughty.

He is standing in front of her; together—the boy, his mother, the cart—they block the narrow sidewalk. A wall right, parked cars left, so she says *boa tarde*, her voice uneven, as if from disuse. The boy continues to rub his belly with one hand and says something she can't make out. He is indifferent to her, unable to understand she has spoken two words in his language. Good evening, she repeats. She steadies herself with one hand against the wall and even thinks to give him some money but remembers she doesn't understand the currency that has changed since the last time she was here. He laughs something she again doesn't understand, pulls on the long handles of the cart. The contents shift. Stepping over a trickle of sewage, Zoë walks on, the cart receding into creaks of accusation.

She returns from the street with a few purchases: underwear, a T-shirt, a pair of shorts with an asperous texture, some yoghurt, a sugary roll, and a bottle of mineral water. Her missing suitcase is there, propped against the unattended front desk. Reaching into a pigeonhole behind the counter, she takes her room key but the suitcase is too heavy for her. Zoë climbs the stairs without it, holding the banister and, after resting on the bed for what seems a long time, calls downstairs. The boy from last night answers and she makes a great effort to speak, to find words and form sentences. She asks if please, if he wouldn't mind, if he could take upstairs the suitcase that is hers and that is in the lobby, at the corner of the desk.

He seems to understand everything she has said, to have no idea that in the street she had felt herself walking slightly above the elevation of her body, a body now collapsed across pilling sheets. She speaks as if she were merely addressing a young man who works the evening and night shift at the front desk of a hotel where the form of a sleeping figure merges at night with the gray vinyl couch, and a calendar is opened to an unlikely month and year. Within a few moments the boy is standing at the door with the suitcase.

"*A senhora foi à praia hoje?*" he asks.

She looks at him, confused.

"Did you go to the beach today?" he repeats, only this time more loudly.

"No, *fui não*."

"Would you like me to take you tomorrow?"

"*Obrigada, amanhã tenho um compromisso* . . . Thank you, tomorrow I have an appointment." An appointment or a commitment? Her words a tattered phrasebook.

If she wants to go tomorrow, he will take her.

Tomorrow *também não posso*. I cannot.

**THAT NIGHT** Zoë doesn't go out. She showers and then lies naked across the bed, picking at the tiny loaf of sweet bread she bought at the bread shop but that she eventually abandons on the bedside table. In a short while, two narrow trails of ants attracted by the sugary crumbs file to and from the bread. The ants carry crumbs almost as large as their own bodies and she jerks to a sitting position, resolved to throw the bread out the window. Looking outside, she remembers she is naked and the light is on. She closes the curtain again, switches off the light but now can't be certain whether tossing the chunk of bread on the sidewalk below will really get rid of the ants; there are still the crumbs on the floor. She throws the big piece out and sprays deodorant on the nightstand and around the floor. In the bathroom, she wets a wad of toilet paper, cleans the table, and experiences a fleeting sense of relief at having contended with an aspect of reality.

When Zoë wakes up, her watch says 8:20. She turns the hands forward one hour. It is evening and a microphone is being tested. The bar next door is beginning to fill up with young people who have parked their motorcycles and cars on the sidewalk. A band is testing the sound equipment. She hadn't noticed the bar, the plastic tables across a cement patio where she now sees the sign: *música ao vivo*.

Hoping to go back to sleep, she takes two tranquilizers but now a woman is singing a ballad, singing but so loudly that the panes rattle in their louvers. She reaches for a tranquilizer and only after a long time falls into a listing sleep from which she is half woken from time to time until the bar closes and it is three o'clock. By four, fully awake, she can no longer stand the thought of being in bed, of being enclosed in a dank bedroom where ants gather around every crumb, but she is afraid to go into the street. She takes the room key and paces up and down the hallway, the cool soundless granite, the flecks of sand that adhere to her bare feet. Not a sound from downstairs, from other guests.

At breakfast she finds the nausea has subsided and she is able to eat some fruit but the voices of two cleaning women arguing in the kitchen echo painfully across her headache. It is just after six in the morning.

By seven, she has paid her bill. She must find somewhere quieter. She tells the taxi driver to take her to Bairro Novo, in Olinda, to a hotel along the waterfront she remembers.

Puddles evaporate into leaden air as the driver edges through the morning traffic, north along the Avenida Boa Viagem. The paved beachside path that was full of strollers an hour ago is now empty-ing but the first bathers are spreading their towels, and men hoping to rent out beach chairs, umbrellas, and body boards arrange their wares across the sand. Two boys bellow popsicle! a fat man strikes a machete against a yellow coconut, a municipal shower drips. The driver manages to pick up speed and at last the air rushes through the open windows. She finds it easier to breathe at that speed. At the end of the stretch that is Recife's failed answer to Copacabana, she sees the entrance to Brasília Teimosa, the promontory taken by the dispossessed who filled in the mangrove swamp, put up their shacks, churches, and brothels, and refused to budge. Stubborn Brasilia.

Crossing the bridge, she can glimpse the rusting carcass of a ship, the warehouses on the other side, and the hesitant skyline of a city that may never boom. There is nowhere to walk on this bridge. Still the people walk, barefoot in bright tattered shorts and tops or else shirtless, indifferent to a traffic that is indifferent to them.

"*O Foro do Recife*," the driver announces. He is pointing at a new building going up on the far side of the river.

"Excuse me?"

"The courthouse. But if it is a palace of justice, only God knows where they'll find the justice to put inside. Here justice belongs to the highest bidder."

A truck rumbles the other direction.

"Money talks," he says, counting out imaginary bills between thumb and forefinger. "We try to teach our children one thing at home, but they learn another in the street. Everyday this city is full of more scoundrels and thieves. If you ask me, there isn't one person here fit to work in that palace. Corruption is in our blood. The only thing that can help you here is family—family and friends."

Brazil may be one of the few places on earth, Zoë thinks to herself, where it is possible to socialize by saying nothing more than "ah," "é? . . . is that right?" or simply nodding one's head every so often. For people to talk endlessly, it is enough to show occasional signs of not having drifted off to sleep. And so, encouraged by nothing but the occasional exchange of a glance in the mirror, the man holds forth about the Virgin, the drought in the backlands, and the Brazilian penchant for evasion through revelry.

"If it all depended on the workings of a system of justice, we would have no hope," he says, circling back to the origin of his monologue. "Here money talks. Any criminal with money, a lot of money, gets off. Meanwhile, the streets are full of bandits pointing guns at the heads of people like me. The only thing that's more dangerous than being a taxi driver is trying to outsmart the devil. *Eu mesmo* . . . Myself, I've been robbed more than seven times, and if I'm here today to tell the story it's because the Lord watches over me. Last week a man got into my car and when he sat down in the front seat I saw the gun at his waist. At that point, what could I do? I couldn't ask him to get out. He noticed I was nervous and he put his hand on his gun and said, 'Don't worry, my business is banks and gas stations.' He wanted to go to the Alto do Pascoal, and I took him there. When we arrived he paid me and walked into a bar. I ask myself, is it worth it? Is it worth it? No one takes taxis here anyway; the rich have their own cars, the poor have two feet."

A one-legged beggar comes up to the window at the next light, but the driver does not need to say the obvious.

The canal separating the opposing lanes of traffic along Agamenon Magalhães is swollen from the rains, and several boys, their
skin glistening, hair dripping, push one another into it, thrash their
way back out, only to hungrily dive back in. At a red light, other
children crowd around the taxi. One of them wants to wash the
windshield. Three others hold out supplicating hands. The welter
of shacks that is the backside of Santo Amaro has filled in slightly
but across from the old Tacaruna factory stands a new shopping
mall in the place of the expanse of shacks that used to be there.
A gargantuan block of windowless concrete, a three-story parking
structure, an air-conditioning unit on the roof. But once they pass
this bit of the first world, the old city of Olinda rises in front of them
on the hill, steeples piercing the luxuriance of breadfruit trees, palm
fronds, and vines. It was the old city that Zoë had thought of when
over the years a part of her had longed to return to Brazil: the crumbling white-washed walls, terracotta rooftops, cobble-stoned streets,
the hue and cry of chickens and, through lattice windows, grand-
mothers dozing on the sofa, the Olinda that is now home to artists,
the disaffected, the flotsam and jetsam of European hippiedom,
the poor and rich living in the rubble of what was once the home
of sugar barons and inquisitors, the Olinda where money doesn't
separate the haves from the hungry so unequivocally. In the Church
of São Bento, the Savior is nailed to the balustrade and faces not the
pews of well-to-do parishioners or the altar but the beggars outside.

The wind is rushing through her hair as the old city grows larger.
To the right, she sees the "five-heart" motel Praia do Norte, to the
left what remains of the coconut grove, the last swath of green separating Recife from Olinda. And then the smell of raw sewage that
announces the canal at the southern border of the Ilha do Maruim,
the slum where the house with the satellite antenna belongs to a
drug trafficker and barefoot children play in the puddles along rut-
ted muddy streets that, according to the maps at city hall, have been
paved and repaved several times. More sex motels, Miami on the
right, Fetiche on the left. She had once found herself in one of these
motels. You drive in, park, pull the half door over the private garage
and enter a temple that is rented by the hour. In the center, like a

fallen altar, a bed, and all around the devotional paraphernalia of the trade: vibrators, KY Jelly, condoms in various colors and flavors, edible underwear, masks, plastic handcuffs, every item priced as marked. Off to one side, like an enormous baptismal font, free to every parishioner and consumer, the Jacuzzi.

As they pass a shop awning she remembers it is a place where the children she had studied often slept. Have the boys she once knew lived to be young men? Against her better judgment, she watches to see if she can spot any familiar children in the street.

If they were at the top of the Old City, looking from the Alto da Sé, the See Hill, the highest peak in the old city, Recife would be a patchwork of wharves, stunted skyscrapers, disheveled huts amid the swampy inlets, and the air would blow fresh from an ocean that past the offing stretches to Nigeria, an air that dries the sweat of the climb. But they are at the foot of the Old City, and the market walls have been painted a different yellowing shade of white. Taxi drivers sleep in their cars but at the Praça do Jacaré children in uniforms wait to cross the street to the parochial school. No one with just enough money would send their children to a public school. Of course, most families don't have just enough, so theirs languish in boredom and neglect at schools where eleven-year-olds can't read and the teachers are irritable from hunger.

A bit further on, the tiny post office at Carmo still recalls a time when letters were written by hand. Where else in the world, Zoë thinks to herself, can you see the ocean behind the man who sells you aerogrammes? She wonders if in this era of e-mail, the post office has lost any of its allure. Just as quickly she decides it must have gained. True letters are the product of a slow gestation. And the lapse in time between their writing and being read means that the author may not be in every sense the person whose writing the recipient struggles to decipher. In that way, while the letter emerges from a quality of intimacy, it also has a life of its own, one that transcends its author.

Then they are driving along the water, past Luar de Prata, the restaurant where many times she had taken the short ride from her apartment to drink cold beer and listen to the water. She had seen a woman there once that she might have fallen in love with. Zoë was alone but the woman with gently curving shoulders was clutching the arm of a man with two chins and a shiny scalp. Later, much later, she would come to know and befriend the woman, Fátima.

SINCE ARRIVING at the Samburá nine days ago, she has contacted no one. Having eaten almost nothing, she doubts she has parasites but wonders if someone could be poisoning her, lacing the water with innervating powders, hallucinogenic drops. She has no appetite but sometimes makes an effort to pick at a slice of bread, swallow a spoonful of yoghurt. Still, she can keep none of it down. She is afraid of the heat, feels a tightness around her lungs, longs for silence. The tranquilizers hardly have any effect now and the worried unease is every bit as intense as if the pilot had just announced that someone was pointing a gun to his head. Only it is an anxiety that has nothing to do with pilots or guns or airplanes. Angst undirected and the world beyond the hotel walls only confirms the impossibility of situating herself in a place her body reached in a matter of hours but that her mind will not assimilate. There is no comfort in not being the woman outside the window who is picking through the trash, who expectantly lifts the lid on the almost empty bin. The few times she has ventured out of the hotel, whether to get some fresh air in the evening or to buy something at the pharmacy or the bread shop, she makes an enormous effort to appear to be what she is: a guest at a hotel, a foreigner who happens to keep to herself. She doubts anyone believes the charade.

Colors look different to her and the bent notes of every vehicle speeding down the road are directed against her. There are ants in this hotel as well. Not only ants but also insects that eat at the entrails of the closet doors, leaving small piles of dust or excrement, she isn't certain.

Decomposition, you could call it an obsession. With her eyes open or shut, in vivid nervous dreams or sedated wakefulness, everywhere there are the putrefying bodies, fetid skin loose on the bones, worm-eaten. Hamlet knew it: *We fat ourselves for maggots.* Life is that willing suspense of disbelief possible only when we blind ourselves to what is coming, to what has already happened, to what is happening at the instant. Thirty thousand children perish each day from malnutrition and diseases that could be treated with primitive medicines. Zoë looks at the clock and tries to calculate the number of babies who die in the time it takes the second hand to make the voyage from the top of the dial to the bottom, but she can't negotiate the division. Brazilians know a faster form of death. The country's toll from murder rivals that from cancer and heart disease. A choice between a bullet and a tumor, a knife and an unsuccessful angioplasty is not a difficult one. A place of stealth, floating on a brackish foundation, canals where you can find poisoned mollusks, faded plastic bottles, and perhaps the body of someone who crossed someone. Much as she tries, she has no recollection of ever having been well. If only she could sleep.

**SOMEONE HAD THE IDEA** of fixing up the hotel but lost the drive or ran out of money. The shelves and clothing rod have been removed from the closet, part of the carpet has been taken up, there are only glue smudges where a mirror was to have gone, above the bathroom sink. Her appearance has been transformed; of that she is certain. But too tired to climb a single flight of stairs, one day she takes the elevator. As the door lurches closed, she is astounded by the image in the mirror: nothing in her eyes, cheeks, or lips hints at the maelstrom that is her mind. She lifts a finger and threads a strand of hair behind one ear. For a long time she stands with a foot in the door, staring at her own reflection, uncertain whether the discrepancy between mind and body is reassuring or only the guarantee that the problem is of another nature.

Sometimes she looks out the window, not wanting, though half expecting, to see one of the street children she had come to know so well in that neighborhood. She had lived less than a mile away. Charles, Buiu, Jalbe, Elvis, Jameson, Ronaldo, Marconi, and, lest she forget, Beto—boys who slept in abandoned cars, under shop awnings, who begged and cajoled their way into breakfast and lunch, who broke into houses at night to steal, who made her laugh. From time to time, she sees children carrying bottles of mineral water or soda they have filled with glue, but she doesn't recognize any of them.

Most of the time she is in bed. If she takes enough tranquilizers she can fall into a hollow sleep but invariably she wakens jittery, flushed, unable to shake the feeling of falling slowly. She rubs her hands together and after a few days of this they are smooth and shiny. She stands, sits, stands, sits or else paces between the bathroom and the far wall. Sometimes she takes her disquiet into the hallway. This hotel is also mostly empty but she has seen a few other guests. For that reason she tends to pace in the hallway only when no one else is around, never before the maids have left for the day, at around two.

In the evenings a curious thing al-
most always happens. A weight lifts
and she is reminded what it is like to
be sane. It is a teasing sensation to
be sure; she has lived the pattern for
enough days to know that it is only
a taste of what life could be like, of
what it was once like. The vague sense of wellness is only fleeting. After observing the pattern for several days she wonders if her condition is called schizophrenia. Forgetting how to tie your shoes must have a name.

One day, she tries to call a friend in New York, a doctor, but after dialing just a few numbers she hears a rapid busy signal. She tries again, with the same result. After a third unsuccessful attempt, Zoë dresses and unsteadily descends to the ground floor where the receptionist tells her it isn't possible to call *lá*, or there, from the hotel. *O dono não permite* . . . the owner doesn't allow it. Zoë bursts into tears. The girl stares at her, uncertain whether to laugh or seek the advice of a higher authority. Tears stream down the foreigner's cheeks, an unquiet weeping. A maid comes over and announces the obvious: *a moça está passando mal*, something is wrong with the young woman. The news makes Zoë irate. Of course something is wrong. The man who cleans the pool walks in barefoot, trailing water. He overheard the exchange and tells Zoë there is a Telemar center she can call from.

"Telemar?" she says, confused less by the suggestion than at the sight of a bare chest that seems to hint at the organs and viscera inside.

"It's a place with telephones. People go there and make phone calls," he explains, clenching an imaginary receiver. He wants to take her there. The man is amused by her insistence on going by herself and tries to explain the way. Unable to understand, she finally allows him to lead her.

Having gotten her to the phone center, the pool cleaner now seems at a loss, suddenly self-conscious about his bare chest and feet. He tells her he will wait outside. Zoë asks the woman at the counter to turn on the meter at one of the phones, and in booth number 3 she manages to complete the call on the first attempt. Only no one picks up. Three rings, four, then a voice on the answering machine. It had never occurred to her that when calling from so far away or with such urgency there might be no one home. Halfway through the recorded message, the first words she has heard in English since arriving in Brazil, she realizes there is no point in speaking to the machine: she doesn't know the number of the hotel. So, at length, she reaches into her bag for the list of telephone numbers from the last time she was in Brazil. Fátima. Fátima will help her.

DOUTOR INÁCIO USHERS HER into his office where the waning afternoon light filters through dusty blinds and, according to the clock that advertises Xanax, it is 4:38. For such a small man, he greets her with an authoritative voice. Dona Zoë, he calls her, and apologizes for the winter rain that has her dress clinging to her body and her hair dripping. He motions for her to sit in the chair on the other side of the desk. She apologizes for having arrived late. She was lost.

"Riverine cities are supposed to be confusing," he decrees. A blue ceramic rhinoceros presides over the desk that separates her from the doctor. "I was once lost in Venice. They say that Recife is the Venice of Brazil but this Venice is nowhere near as confusing as that one. I was a seminary student in Rome when I visited the city at the age of fourteen, and the experience led me to disappoint my mother and not become a priest. For one thing I realized that Recife was made no more in the image of Venice than man was in the image of God. But *mais ainda* . . . more importantly, God was unable to lead me back to my group of fellow students who by five in the afternoon had already left without me."

The rhinoceros stands atop a pile of yellowing papers.

Doutor Inácio clears his throat. "Dona Fátima has told me that you were not feeling well."

She lifts her eyes from the paperweight to the glint off his glasses. There is an endearing intensity to this man who is too tightly contained inside a small frame.

"I need to rest," she says simply.

He looks at her, holding his pen aloft.

"I cannot sleep."

He is still looking at her.

"I need stronger tranquilizers. I can't sleep without taking three or four pills and even then I don't rest. I need to rest."

The psychiatrist makes some scribbles on a large index card. There is no computer in this office, no Dictaphone visible, no secretary outside. It is just this man's word against an index card.

"There is a storm inside my head that won't let me rest, or think, or tie my shoes properly. I need you to stop it!"

He asks her to lie on the examining table as he listens to her chest, takes her blood pressure, palpates her stomach, and, for no reason she can fathom, shines a light inside her ears. Perhaps, if the problem is in her brain, the closest he can get is through the ears. It has been a long time since someone touched her. She wants to be held by the little man.

"How long have you been taking tranquilizers?" he wants to know.

"I need to rest."

"At what time do you wake up in the morning?"

"By four."

"At what time do you wake up when you are at home?"

"At six or seven."

"What was the first thing you would do in the morning, when you were here before?"

"Walk along the beach."

"Do you do that now?"

"I don't walk now," she mumbles, holding back the fact that the sight of the sea is strangely menacing to her, that the city as a whole has provoked in her something like an allergic reaction. Yes, perhaps it is the city, everything about it. She feels as hemmed in as when the door of the airplane that brought her here closed. She must get out of the office, out of the city. Only there is nothing comforting about the thought of changing her ticket, getting on a plane, and returning to a city where she has no place to live because there is a tenant in her apartment: a man paying her rent, eating at her table, sleeping in her bed, soiling her sheets.

He asks if she won't step up on the scale. When they make the conversion from kilos to pounds she is surprised to find she's lost fifteen pounds but also inwardly struck that there is any substance left to her at all.

"I have to rest," she insists, the tears welling up in her eyes, making the book-lined walls a welter of fading colors. She walks over to the wall and picks up a volume that happens to have nothing to do with psychiatry, an old edition of a novel by Machado de Assis. She puts it down, picks it up, puts it down, opens its pages, closes them. The chaos of it all, the spines of so many books in so many colors, the books at odd angles, words written by a dead author, the rusting paper clips that have no place on a bookshelf. A hand on her back and she cannot contain the scream.

When she leaves the office at just after six, the sidewalks and streets behind the Catholic University teem with workers returning home. She decides to fill the prescription at the nearest pharmacy rather than at the one around the corner from her hotel in Olinda. In a city where drugstores are almost as plentiful as street corners, it is no surprise that within a block or two she comes across the yellow and red sign of the misnamed Farmácia dos Pobres, the Pharmacy of the Poor. She passes that one by, walks one street up to Conde da Boa Vista and enters a Pague Menos. Pay Less. At first there are a few people at the counter. A woman is asking what to do about a rash on her arm. The man behind the counter finds her some cream, which she looks at but decides she doesn't want. When it is Zoë's turn and the man receives the blue slip of paper from her hand, he first looks at it upside down, then right-side up. He seems to be squinting. He holds it for a long time before showing it to a man who says some-thing Zoë cannot hear over the traffic outside. Finally they begin rummaging through little boxes arranged in alphabetical order, by product name.

"Sertralina, 50 mg.," reads the label.

For a long time Zoë hesitates before opening her purse and taking out her wallet. The month's supply of antidepressants costs the equivalent of fifty dollars. With what right, she wonders, in a city where entire families must live for a month on less than the cost of a box of imported pills? The thought has a physical consistency, smarts like a disturbed wound. What comes to mind at that moment is a pallet. More than any other detail, that is what struck her about the visit she once made to the home of two brothers who washed windshields near the Hospital da Restauração. Bags of rice sewn together and stuffed with the crumpled pages of newspapers served as the family's sole bed. Was fifty dollars enough to buy a cheap mattress?

The boy, his words on a cassette she still kept, said: "Sometimes we haven't come up with any money, so we stay here, in the street. We crumple up some newspaper and lay it down on the sidewalk. Or else we crawl into an empty pipe. In there, with a lot of newspaper, it isn't so bad. Once, we were somewhere where there were no pipes and it was raining. My brothers and I went into a telephone booth, the four of us, and we fell asleep there, standing up, falling over one another. When you know the street, you can sleep anywhere."

Zoë had had a great-grandmother on her father's side who spent her final years in a mental hospital, convinced that her son, who visited her on weekends, was an impostor sent by the king of Spain. Schizophrenia, people say, might be hereditary. But schizophrenia was not her only suspicion. She wondered if she might not be addicted to the tranquilizers. The latter fear turned out to be true but Doutor Inácio had called the larger problem depression, not schizophrenia. She did not know that with depression you could leave your body, hear voices, perceive the changing hues of monuments.

She has trouble counting the money and lays the bills out on the counter, unable to make sense of them, of the situation. The box of pills so tiny next to the thought of a bed or a few bags of groceries. She remembers her credit card. The assistant tells her they will have to charge an extra five percent if she uses the card. She gives it to him anyway, pushing the confusion of notes back into her purse.

Faltering from the shop onto a sidewalk crowded with the metal tables and chairs that accompany every luncheonette in Brazil and that advertise one brand or another of beer, the city center, it seems to her, is a cauldron of chaos and decay, the physical manifestation of her mind. The air is heavy with exhaust and the smell of fried foods. Unable to shake the sensation of walking through her own consciousness, of revisiting a chapter of the past from which all references to herself—a character who in any case had never belonged—were long ago excised, she walks toward the bus stop on the Rua do Hospicio, on the edge of the park, but changes her mind when she sees the crowd of people waiting for the Olinda and Rio Doce lines.

She turns the other way, hoping there is still a taxi rank on the far side of the Law Faculty, on the Rua da Princesa. Rounding the corner of the Faculty, it is as if she had heard her name called out in a distant falsetto, two syllables that barely carry. She wonders what it means that evening in Recife is as she remembers it: distrustful women holding their purses to their chests, pensioners looking over their shoulders, a barefoot boy being detained by the police, unsmiling civil servants lining up for buses that will take them to muddy suburbs. A rain, light at first, begins to fall. Strange, she thinks, because rain is almost never a casual affair in this city. It is either pouring or not raining at all. Across the street an old woman with a foot bloated and heavy from elephantiasis lurches on. Thinking the voice is inside her head, Zoë doesn't turn. Umbrellas unfold. But then, unmistakably, from closer this time, the same call. She turns.

Near the people scurrying for cover under the trees because the rain, as it turns out, is not going to be casual but fierce, she makes out a tall silhouette moving toward her with strides of arrested femininity, the fulgence of a street lamp glinting up and down scarred forearms, a head of thick black hair.

"*Você voltou, foi?* . . . So you've come back?" The figure says this winded, not quite smiling. The figure is standing there in a white blouse, shirttails knotted together just above the navel, tight jeans, black plastic heels. Zoë assumes she has been mistaken for someone else, but nonetheless squints uncomfortably.

"*Quis saber mais sobre a cultura pernambucana, foi?* . . . You wanted to know more about the culture of Pernambuco?" The figure says.

Some passersby step widely around the twosome. The odd thing is the sense of recognition emerging from within the unreality. What a strange question. And the hurried sound of drops pattering the leaves in the park. It is something about the figure's hair. And the eyes.

"Beto?" she says, finally.

"Beto died."

"Beto died?"

"My name is Aparecida."

"I don't know any Aparecida," Zoë says, turning to escape her own confusion. Zoë begins to walk away, but then the figure says something she cannot ignore: "I remember the chalk."

"The chalk?"

"Do you remember it?"

"What do you mean?"

"You gave me chalk, so I could draw on the walls of the abandoned house."

"Beto?"

"Beto died. I am Aparecida now. Not Maria Aparecida like all the others, just Aparecida. I just appeared. If you want, I can tell you what we really think."

"Tell me what who thinks?" Zoë says.

"*Nós, os maloqueiros . . .*"

"What the riffraff think . . . ?"

"We think all day long, it's the only thing we do."

"What do you mean Beto died? Which Beto?"

"There were other Betos, on television, but the only Beto I knew in real life has died. I'm Aparecida now."

"Then you are Beto?"

"What did you do with all those voices you took with you?"

"Voices?"

"Yes."

"The tapes? My interviews . . . ?"

"Do you have them?"

"Yes, at home, in my country."

"That's where all of those children are. You won't find them here. That's the only place you'll find Beto. They've all gone."

"Aparecida?"

"Yes?"

Zoë reaches to hug him (hug her?) (hug the figure). Her head falls on Aparecida's bony shoulder, but the embrace is not returned. The body she is embracing is not limp or lifeless, only inaccessible. The feeling of being an invisible presence in her own memories shattered, Zoë clings with the little strength she retains. Ribs press against her breasts. When she lets go, she doesn't know what to say. Wetness has gathered in her sandals and in the corners of her eyes.

"*Como vai* . . . How are you doing?" she tries.

"*Vou levando* . . . I am carrying on. And you?"

An old man pulling a two-wheeled cart full of cardboard and plastic bottles passes between them. He moves slowly, oblivious to the falling water. Does it matter that the cardboard is getting wet?

"I'm also carrying on."

"I didn't think I would see you again."

"I've come back." Zoë wipes one cheek, looks toward but not quite at the neoclassical dome atop the Law Faculty. The Law Faculty. Once the site where the elite of Northeast Brazil were trained, now homeless people lounge in the manicured gardens.

"How are the others?" That is the only thing that occurs to Zoë to say but she regrets the words as soon as she has uttered them. Aparecida has already told her why she can't ask that question.

"What others?"

"Your friends."

"In the street we don't have friends."

Beto's cheekbones . . . Aparecida's cheekbones. They are high, but high in slightly different ways. Is it true what they say about the transvestites here, that they inject one another with industrial silicone: wide hips, generous buttocks, sculpted lips? Perhaps the silicone in her cheeks has shifted. The names of other street children come to her and Zoë says one. "Margarete?"

"I told you. They are on your tapes. That is where you will find them."

"On the tapes?"

Aparecida seems to have reconsidered. "Margarete disappeared a long time ago. Some people say she went to Bahia. Before that, she was in Tamarineira. She had three children and the children were taken away from her . . . to Switzerland, or else to São Paulo. When the last one was taken away Margarete undressed and walked naked in the streets. She covered her body with mud from the river and walked until she was arrested. Margarete suffered from nerves. That was when they put her in Tamarineira. But I think she escaped from there. We don't stay long anywhere. Not even in life, which is why I think she is dead.

"Charles was run over by a bus, one of the blue ones, an electric bus. Afterwards, he was alive but now he carries around his intestines outside his stomach, in a bottle. They are still his intestines, they are still attached to him, it's just that they no longer fit where they used to fit. That's why he carries them in a bottle. The smell is so strong you know he's coming a long time before you see him, which is why he can't steal anymore. But people feel sorry for him and leave him food. I leave him food when I smell him. It brings luck. Once I left him an apple. I smelled him coming and put the apple on a bench by the river. When I came back the apple was gone and that same night I found a bill, ten reais, that someone had dropped on the ground."

"What about Xandre Pequeno?"

"Xandre Pequeno killed Xandre Grande. Then he killed three other people, one at a time. After that, someone killed him."

When Aparecida is done saying who is dead, who is in jail, who is on the same street corner, she asks, "*É bom lá?* . . . Is it good there?"

"Where?"

"*Lá, onde você mora* . . . In that place where you live."

"I don't know."

The answer seems to satisfy Aparecida, whose eyes are the only window onto Beto. And there is an air, something in the spirit of this person that is familiar. But there is another person here as well.

The boy with a shock of bewildered hair and so much timid curiosity is nowhere evident. Aparecida carries herself with assurance and is certain, it would seem, that she is who she wants to be.

"*Foi um prazer revê-la* . . . It was a pleasure to see you again," Aparecida says. The cordiality strikes Zoë as both peculiar and sincere. The brief exchange has reached its conclusion. The boy Zoë had imagined as her son has grown up. He is not dead. They have met again, he is a woman, and now it is time for them to go their separate ways.

"It was a pleasure to see you again," Zoë also says. She is about to leave but turns a last time and says, "Will I see you again?"

"*Fico no bocetão* . . . I stay in the big cunt."

"What?"

"*Fico na rua da Aurora* . . . On Aurora Street. That's where I crochet." Aparecida puts her hand on a peeling black bag slung across her shoulder, a long needle protruding. "*Antes da Ponte do Limoeiro* . . . Before you get to the Limoeiro Bridge."

Zoë remembers the place the children call the big cunt, a clearing at the edge of the river, a hollow like Plato's cave, only the shifting silhouettes are the things of substance.

Aparecida extends the rough hand of a man, the nails of a woman, then walks back in the direction she came from. For her part, Zoë continues slowly the other way. After a few paces, her consciousness swaying, Zoë is overcome with a breathless nausea, the unsteadiness of the street. Her hotel in Olinda seems impossibly far, unreachable now. With both hands she grasps at the iron bars of the fence that surrounds the Law Faculty, the noises of the city receding as the air grows heavier. Still she clings to the fence. She is vomiting now, vomiting furiously through the bars, vomiting a burning white liquid. The final drops dangle from her chin. She doesn't faint but knows herself to be falling. She must sit, sit; better yet, lie, feel against her cheeks the pavement of a receding city.

DOUTOR INÁCIO HAD SAID it may take a few weeks for the antidepressants to take effect. With the second hand on her watch hardly advancing, the idea of a few weeks strikes Zoë as incomprehensible. While she feels a sense of disbelief that anything like a box of pills could help her condition, the possibility that this might be a chemical imbalance in the brain, as Doutor Inácio had suggested ("some people suffer from high blood pressure, others from depression"), gives her a tenuous feeling of hope. Doutor Inácio had urged her not to discuss her condition with other people.

For almost a week after her visit to his office, she feels a little better, as if the fog were beginning to dissipate slightly. Is that the placebo effect, the comfort of receiving a diagnosis?

She sometimes manages to sleep for several hours during the heat of the day and regains some of her appetite. For five days, she does not vomit. After that, everything she had felt before is only accentuated: the nausea, the hot flashes, the weight in her chest and against her lungs, the need to pace from one side of the room to the other. The unbearable sensitivity to sound, the rejection of her surroundings, the stormy chatter in her brain, the feeling that she is rarely inside her body.

Fátima stops by almost every day and continues to insist that Zoë stay with her. Zoë wishes she wouldn't. The visits leave her exhausted, as if the effort required to hold a brief conversation called for a force of concentration inaccessible to her.

If this is depression, as Doutor Inácio had decreed after a single visit to his office, of one thing she is certain: the small man with beady eyes has never experienced anything like this. The greatest danger of depression, he had said, is suicide. The greatest danger, Zoë knows, is the condition itself. Aside from those moments in the afternoon when the weight lifts, when she has a tenuous sensation of peace, the thought of suicide is her sole relief. It is a fantasy that allows her to transcend a withering body and careening mind, the world where the same woman passes by each afternoon to examine the rubbish in the street. She tells herself that, given the noise from the street, she cannot be too close to the window but knows that the noise is not the only reason.

After several weeks a strange thing happens. She can look at the vault of a sky that returns no menace. The noises from the street are less acute. She can bear the sight of the sea. She feels almost all right and this in itself strikes her as the most exquisite sensation she has ever experienced. Doutor Inácio's warning had not ended with the words, "The greatest danger of depression is suicide." He completed the sentence, "the greatest danger of the medication is euphoria." She keeps the feeling to herself, savors it.

Something else happens. Fátima phones to say that her friend Tadeo has an apartment for rent. It is in Casa Caiada, not far from where she is staying now. In the evening, they walk together. The air off the water is not brisk but fresh. Zoë stops to look at the light from a gas lantern: a man selling popcorn. Cars with steamed windshields are parked in the darkness here and there. "*Os motéis estão muito caros* . . . The love motels are too expensive," Fátima jokes.

Estrela do Mar is a new sixteen-story building facing the sea. Flanked on all sides by high walls, watched over by dark-skinned men wiry from the hunger that was their childhood, this is the dream of a nearly white parvenu. It has two parking spaces per apartment, a rooftop *salão de festas*, an exercise room, even a tiny sauna for those who prefer to get their heat from an activity other than walking in the open air.

When she sees the building she realizes it stands where there had once been an abandoned house, the one where Beto would draw on the crumbling walls.

Someone on a high floor is playing Frank Sinatra.

Fátima speaks though the intercom to a guard who buzzes them in but then can't find the keys to the apartment. He sifts uselessly through the contents of a drawer in the guard booth: bits of paper, a screwdriver, loose bullets, a leaky ballpoint pen. After a while he gives up and calls upstairs to the *síndico*, who in New York might be called the co-op chair. The breeze off the ocean ripples the surface of the tiny ground-floor swimming pool.

In a few minutes a tall, spare, loose-jointed man appears with the keys. He is circumspect but also seems to like the idea of a foreigner living in the building, as if it might bring some cachet to the place.

"One of the *vereadores* from Igarassú just moved in," he says. Zoë remembers both the dusty misery of the outlying town with its colonial church and the possibilities of personal enrichment available to an elected councilor. "We used to live in Janga," he says, "but we moved here to be closer to the city. *E é uma delícia* . . . It's marvelous to be close to the city but be able to look out and see this." He points to the sea, just beyond what he calls the *menino* cleaning the pool. The "boy" is barefoot, dark-skinned, about forty.

Fátima, Zoë, and the *síndico* enter the elevator. As the doors close, a fan is activated in the ceiling. The *síndico* is pleased with this innovation and he doesn't bother to fix his hair. A note taped to the mirror and signed by him asks residents to use the service elevator if they are returning from the swimming pool or are wearing bathing suits, but someone has scribbled a profanity in the bottom part of the page.

"*Não se respeita mais ninguém nesse nosso Brasil*" . . . No one respects anyone in this Brazil of ours," he laments before Zoë and Fátima step out into the eighth-floor landing.

The apartment has three bedrooms, the invariable minimum for the modern operation of middle-class life. Zoë says she would like to live by the sea but doesn't need so much space. Fátima smiles broadly.

The apartment has never been lived in and the floors are covered with chalky dust. Zoë opens the sliding glass door to the terrace and the kitchen door slams shut with startling force. The trade winds change all the calculations. Clouds of dust have been stirred up. The two women laugh, embrace one another. Fátima threads a strand of Zoë's hair behind her ear.

The master bedroom is the farthest back from the water. Zoë decides that if she takes the apartment, her room will be the small one closest to the sea where a rectangular hole in the wall above the window is meant for an air-conditioner. She likes the hole there, the exposure to the elements.

**THE NEXT DAY** Fátima picks Zoë up at the hotel and helps her move her things into Tadeo's apartment. Fátima has brought some sheets and towels and together they go to buy a mattress, a gas stove, a small refrigerator, pots, pans, and glasses. The stove and the refrigerator will be delivered, the mattress is strapped to the roof of Fátima's car. They forget to buy light bulbs. When they return from the hardware store they realize there are no toilet seats in the bathrooms. Each choice—to leave her books on the floor or buy some boards and cinder blocks, whether or not to get a set of glasses, which model of refrigerator—reignites some ancestral cache of panic, makes Zoë wonder whether she shouldn't have just rented a room in someone's house. She tries to determine how many homeless people could fit inside her apartment, how many children could be fed with the money from her sabbatical pay.

After cleaning the floors, Zoë pushes the mattress into the bedroom closest to the sea and makes it up. The window is small for such a spectacular view. Lying on the floor, she can see the sky not the water. A bed would have to be almost three feet high for a view of the sea. The windows in the living room are likewise small and high, as if the view onto the ocean were a mere coincidence.

The first night Zoë is awakened by a lashing wind and rain. Almost instantly the floor is wet and she must drag her mattress into the living room. She'll have to cover the hole for the air-conditioning unit. For a long time the rain continues to beat down against the sides of the building and the wind whistles around the edges of the windows, underneath the doors. She looks out through the living room windows at the sheets of water glittering down under the floodlights, her loneliness complete.

Early the next morning she realizes she has moved into a building adjacent to two construction sites. To one side, another tall building is being finished. The skeleton is complete but the windows, doors, and tile work are all missing. Behind, a new building is going up. This one rises only five stories but seems poised to grow many more. She is astounded to see odd-shaped tree limbs used as supports for what, for now, is the highest floor; the pillars are thin rectangles of cement and iron rods. She wonders if the building she is in is any more solid.

By seven in the morning, hammers are clinking against tiles, saws are cutting through concrete, a cement mixer is churning. Remembering she has already given her word to Tadeo that she will stay here until she goes home just after New Year's, she knows herself to be trapped.

There had been a comfort in her anonymity at the hotel, in her state of apparent transience. Now she must make a case for her existence, for her having come to Brazil. Day in and day out neighbors will see her. She closes the back windows of the apartment that give onto the busy avenue behind and onto one of the construction sites. The rumble of buses is muffled slightly but the noise of construction persists.

She has not organized herself to the point of cooking. For one thing, when the stove arrives she realizes she has no way of connecting it to the pipe that comes out of the wall. The deliveryman doesn't know how to either and suggests she call the store. This requires leaving the building, buying a phone card, waiting at the public telephone. Just this in the heat of day is more than she can bear. Over the phone, the store manager does not understand her. She hangs up in frustration. The *zelador*, or handyman, at her building says he can do it. He tries, but is unable. For the most part, Zoë eats the same fare of yoghurt, bread, and fruit or else she goes out to one of the new self-serve restaurants where you pay for food by weight. Often she eats at one a short walk south in Bairro Novo where coconut trees, sand, water, and beggars are framed by the open window. She prefers to go before or after the midday rush when attendants from the nearby banks and shops come to eat.

During her first weeks at the apartment, Zoë continues to awaken very early. At that time, before five in the morning, the first walkers have set off along the road in front of the building, which is closed to traffic. She uses the pool. Something about the water, the immersion in another element, calms her. We spend so much time in the air, but almost never return to the water. She begins to feel her best at that time of day, in the pool at dawn.

Every once in a while she revels in the absence of the paralyzing disquiet she felt before. She feels she is beginning to return from a journey she had never intended to make and realizes that there is nothing more depleting than an aversion to life itself. One day she sleeps on and off for eighteen hours. The next day she skips her dawn swim.

Something that strikes her as the deepest sadness she has ever felt sets in where the angst begins to attenuate. This state, melancholy, you could call it, is almost a relief; the panic—at breathing or not breathing, at eating or not eating, at being awake or asleep—the sense that she had forgotten how to fry an egg, was far worse. There is something restorative about a state of complete resignation.

She still has not been in touch with any friends except Fátima. The thought of doing nothing, of frittering away her sabbatical, has an innervating quality to it. Be that as it may, she has lost all interest in the research she had meant to undertake. She had meant to live in a *favela* among working children. In her building, by contrast, the plump children she sometimes meets in the elevator vacation in Orlando.

The terrace is the quietest part of the apartment. A rectangular box facing the sea, it has two hooks mounted on the walls to either end. Zoë spends the bulk of her time suspended in a hammock. The anti-psychotic medication prescribed by Doutor Inácio on a second visit has her sleeping much of the time and groggy when awake. But when she is slightly more alert, she observes what can be seen from her terrace: the sea's changing hues of blue and green speckled here and there with floating plastic debris, the small waves cresting against the breakwater a couple hundred yards from the shore. A few people venture into the water, but most know better—it isn't necessary to walk far in one direction or the other to find a small stream of sewage trickling into the ocean.

When the tide is high, the gentle waves almost reach the pavement below her building but there is a wide swath of beach off to the right. Unless it is raining, by early in the morning and until about half past five when night falls with equatorial resolve, the sand is a patchwork of umbrellas, towels, and shimmering bodies. She uses the pair of binoculars she brought to get a closer look. There is something pleasing about the insouciance with which aging women display their bodies, she thinks to herself one day, bringing into focus a woman who stands arms akimbo and watching over two children digging a hole in the sand. The woman's thighs and belly are rippled with age and extra weight. She wears a *fio dental*—dental floss bikini—the top half of which is two small triangles attached by strings. Band-Aids to cover the nipples. Why the nipples? she wonders. What is sacred about them? Zoë's gaze falls on a man in a pair of swimming trunks that almost disappear below the protrusion of his belly. The body may be an obsession here, a constant source of temptation and of wishful thinking, but it is not to be hidden, it is not a hindrance.

The first time she came to Brazil it was to study the street but now Zoë lives in a building designed to protect its inhabitants from the street. The sixteen-story tower is a walled compound watched over day and night by men who earn just a little more than minimum wage, about a hundred dollars per month. For the most part, unless they are walking early in the morning, residents come and go only by car. A man from the eleventh floor wants to rent the two parking spaces that came with her apartment. She is the only person in the building without an automobile.

Parents let their children play freely on the ground-floor terrace, even around the pool, but not outside the compound. There is an exodus from the building in the mornings just after seven when mothers drive their children to school and fathers and some of the mothers leave for work.

Zoë doesn't have a key to her building. The other residents don't either. There's no need. When arriving home by car from work or a trip with the kids to the shopping mall, residents flash their lights or honk and one svelte, dark-skinned man or another presses a button and the door to the parking garage slides open. Drawn slowly to one side by a hydraulic lever, the door brings the medieval drawbridge up to date, separating the late-twentieth-century downsized castle and its nouveau-almost-riche apartment dwellers from the perils of the world beyond.

Since Zoë doesn't have a car, she enters and leaves the building by foot. When she returns from the street, she presses a button in the hope of being buzzed in. So far it has always worked. These *boys*—to be faithful to the local nomenclature—are charged not only with letting the residents in and out but also with guarding their domestic safety. They have a gun somewhere in the smoked glass turret that, from the outside, doesn't allow one to know where the guard's gaze is trained. It is that uncertainty, of course, that makes this a safe building. Aside from the turret and the guard, the block of flats relies on the barrier method: high walls topped with coils of razor wire.

The chart posted by the elevator details expenses in the building. The wages for the guards and the custodians are, taken together, slightly less than the cost of the communal water bill.

There seems to be strife in the building. Zoë gathers this from the agenda for the next resident's meeting, which is slid under her door one day. One item of discussion is the use of radios around the pool. The *síndico* wants to ban this practice but it is clear that many disagree. On weekends, a number of residents gather around the pool to drink Johnny Walker Red, sweat, and listen to Frank Sinatra at a volume that overpowers even the construction from next door.

What is it about northeastern men of a certain class that makes them so fond of Frank Sinatra? And of car racing? The salesman who visited Zoë in her apartment had tried to entice her into taking out a subscription to the *Jornal do Commércio* by allowing her to choose between two complimentary items—the Greatest Hits of Frank Sinatra or a commemorative Ayrton Senna calendar. She paid for the subscription but told the man he could save the gifts for someone else.

Lacking the concentration to read anything of substance, it suits her to study the local paper. After a few days she finds there is something like a formula. The front page is reserved for soccer, violent crime, or charges of corruption. A gang of six or seven armed and masked men overpowered the two guards at the entrance to a love motel and went from room to room, stealing valuables, cell phones, and every stitch of clothing from the distracted occupants of the rooms. With the security guards tied up, the front gates to the motel barricaded, and the guests naked and penniless but not in the company of their spouses, the crime was not discovered for hours. Elsewhere in the city, a boy who didn't want to surrender his Nikes was shot in the stomach and an elderly woman was mugged shortly after cashing her pension check, for the third consecutive month.

The row in the building over the use of radios around the pool is nothing compared with the one over a statue commissioned for kilometer zero in Old Recife. The planning committee had awarded the contract to the eccentric millionaire ceramist Brennand, who was asked to design the monument as he saw fit. This one, when the maquette was completed, turned out to be as phallic as every other statue the man ever made, only far larger than any seen before. A barely disguised sixty-foot erection was too much for some, but no one will take responsibility for having nixed the idea. After all, in any moneyed house in Recife you can find tiles and a few garden sculptures by Brennand. A journalist at the *Diário de Pernambuco* pins the blame on the mayor's wife, who is a member of the city's planning committee. Brennand vows to never accept another commission from the city. The mayor, a former professor of constitutional law and suddenly the target of endless ridicule, denies any involvement on the part of his wife in the decision to rescind the contract. But that is not all. He is said to walk into the offices of the paper and hold an unregistered gun to the head of the offending journalist. The peace is made with Brennand, who is prevailed upon to carry on with his work. The mayor has balls, the city will have its erection.

The paper reserves page twelve for *O Mundo*. One day the international news is as follows: (1) The Ukraine is considering implementing a program of banking reform; (2) Michael Jackson has collapsed onstage in Thailand and canceled his concerts in Singapore and Malaysia; (3) a doctor in Colorado has come up with a new and less invasive surgical procedure for liposuction. More than a thousand miles from any international border, Pernambuco has a sense of self unlike anywhere Zoë has ever been. Poor people, who are most people in this state, may not have heard of the United States or know that São Paulo, Brazil's largest city, is in fact in Brazil.

Something has changed since the last time she was here, Zoë knows, without even having to leave the terrace. For one thing, there are suddenly a lot of fat people. In *Veja*, Brazil's version of *Time* magazine, she comes across an article that says that in 1975 there were two to four cases of malnutrition for every case of obesity. By 1996 the relationship was inverted. A revolution. The marriage of fat and famine hosted by a single population: the poor. Coca-Cola, lard, popcorn, beans, "French" bread leavened with chemicals; the amount one takes in determines the girth. The president, once a Marxist intellectual, is proud that in this nation of toothless people, so many can now afford dentures. And then there is the fact that cell phones ring on buses.

**AS ON EVERY SUNDAY AFTERNOON,**
drunken men and women dance to
tinny radios. Strewn across the sand
and sidewalks and streets are crumpled
plastic cups, straws, cigarette butts,
coconut husks. It is a Sunday afternoon
when Zoë decides to leave her apartment
and go back into the city. Almost two

months have passed since she collapsed outside the Law Faculty.

There is little traffic so the ride has barely taken fifteen minutes
when she pulls on the knotted cord. With the noise, Zoë cannot hear
if the bell near the driver has rung but the bus stops abruptly in
front of the evangelical church on Cruz Cabugá. Walking through
the early afternoon loneliness of the Rua do Lima, she sees, through
half-shuttered windows, men sleeping off lunch and empty bottles
while the women, languid, resigned, clear the last dishes before
themselves retiring to the sofa or a hammock. As she walks, Zoë
feels as out of place as if her presence were itself a foreign object.

Reaching the Rua da Aurora, the broad avenue that runs along
the Capibaribe River, she sees a man looking through the window
of what is left of a certain building, pieces of the façade and a few
girders. The man is looking out the window. Beneath a ceiling that
rises to the sky and framed amid the shock of green that sprouts in
every part of the city not smothered beneath the asphalt, he watches
her, his eyes on her back as she makes her way across the avenue.
She pauses between the stones that form the median. There are no
cars in sight up or down the avenue. In the vacant lot on the other
side of the street, discarded machinery rusts on the aging, cracked
pavement and shards of broken bottles glint amid the pebbles. The

air is thick with the smell of sewage in the river. There is another smell. She turns and sees the cooking fire. A man of unguessable age is sitting on a log. Next to him, a woman, her belly swollen with a baby or perhaps just swollen, tends the fire, her knotted hair rising in strange peaks.

When the man turns to Zoë, he reveals the pale shade of pink where his front teeth are missing and asks for money. Before she can lie that she has none, he asks for pills, a drink, a cigarette, the ante spiraling downward.

"I am looking for Aparecida."

His face changes. He stops asking for things, stops talking, looks away.

"Do you know her?"

He doesn't reply.

"She said I could find her here. That's what she told me when I saw her by Treze de Maio, she said she stayed around here."

"What does she look like?" he says, with disinterest.

"She's a transvestite, she has hair down to here." Zoë touches her shoulders.

"*É pobrema?*" he asks, transposing the *r* and skipping the *l* of *problema*. He is suspicious. Zoë wonders what she looks like to him, wonders if the eyes of the man behind her, across the street, are still trained on her back, if some day the city might not again become a forest.

"No. It's nothing like that."

"Why do you want her?" he asks.

Is he taking her for some sort of a client?

"I just want to talk with her," she mumbles, realizing the truth often makes for an unimpressive answer. "No, it isn't trouble. She was expecting me."

Slowly the toothless man directs his gaze toward the lamppost and the chunk of upturned cement at the border between the vacant lot and the mangrove trees, "*Olhe ela ali!* Look at her there."

**ZOË APPROACHES** the sleeping figure whose mouth is slightly agape. Aparecida's hair obscures her face but doesn't cover the mutilated lobe from which more than one earring must have been yanked off. She is wearing more masculine clothing this time, jeans and a T-shirt, but has clips in her hair. Even in her sleep she is clutching the black knapsack. The boy who drew on walls. Zoë is about to walk away, embarrassed to wake Aparecida, when the woman tending the fire yells out, *Bicha maluca*! Aparecida lurches upright, dropping the small tattered knapsack to the ground, its contents spilling: a ball of yarn, crochet needles, a fragment of a broken mirror, lipstick, an empty mineral water bottle, a pen. There is something demented about the way the toothless man and the woman are laughing.

Aparecida, sullen, gathers her things, pushing them back into her bag and smoothes her hair. "*Tudo bem*, Zoë . . . How are things?"

"Fine, fine. And you?"

"*Vou bem* . . . I'm well."

"I was wondering if you would like to talk with me."

Aparecida doesn't seem to find anything strange about the suggestion, so Zoë asks if they shouldn't walk to another part of the park.

As they make their way along the river, toward the Monumento Tortura Nunca Mais, the Torture Never Again Monument, Aparecida stumbles. At first Zoë thinks she is high but then that she is just sleepy. In the end, she isn't certain. They walk past the dusty soccer field where barefoot boys are chasing a dirty

ball. The sun is still strong but there is wind, as there always is when the tide is high. The river, which meets the sea not far from there, is swollen.

Reaching the monument, they sit in the half shade of the enormous figure of a man left to hang perpetually in an inverted fetal position. The statue is a memorial to political prisoners who were tortured under the more than two decades of dictatorship the country suffered before the restoration of democracy. Yet it has a more contemporary meaning, it had always seemed to Zoë: the petty thieves, street children, and common criminals continue to be tortured in this manner in police stations and prisons.

There is something stolid, masculine about Aparecida's hands and feet. But her high cheekbones, her hair, above all her gaze, are womanly. Her voice a man's, the sweep of her hair to one side that of a young girl.

Zoë begins to explain. She explains that she is spending half a year in Brazil this time and that she had the idea to write a book about Aparecida's life. Zoë doesn't quite know how to put it. "I would like to talk with you, to record our conversations, to write about your life, together."

"I would need to fill up two notebooks, is that it?" Aparecida says.

"You know how to write?"

"Yes."

"When did you learn how to write?"

"I knew when I was still Beto."

"Why didn't you tell me?"

There is no answer from Aparecida.

"Then that would be a good idea," Zoë says finally.

Zoë suggests that if she manages to publish anything they could share the royalties. She also says she could pay for the interviews. There is something apologetic in her manner, in her choice of words.

"Whatever you think."

"No, we need to think about this together."

"If you think so."

"I can't promise you I can publish anything. But we can try. Maybe if it isn't a book, we can prepare an essay, something short." She wonders if Aparecida knows what an essay is.

"That doesn't matter."

"Of course it matters, but we'll try."

Aparecida says nothing.

"Would you like to do an interview now?"

"*Agora?*"

"Yes, now, unless . . ."

"All right."

"All right, then."

"Do you have a cigarette?"

"No."

"Will you buy me one?"

"Yes."

"Dona Digna sells cigarettes." Aparecida points at the little kiosk next to the service station.

When Zoë returns, Aparecida is surprised to be offered a whole pack rather than a single cigarette. She at first accepts only one.

"It's all right, I quit," Zoë says.

"I used to have many vices, now this is my only one."

"Do you miss the other vices?"

"You can start asking the questions. I know how to answer."

But once Zoë has turned on the tape recorder, Aparecida does not wait for questions. With a voice that is neither a boy's nor a woman's, which addresses not Zoë but the tape recorder, she is having a conversation with a small machine. Unmistakable now the smell of glue on her breath, Aparecida speaks fragments:

*Those spirits that wander about today were once angels, angels who organized a rebellion in the sky, a rebellion against the will of God. Because in the Bible it says that God made the world in three days, in three days? And on the next day God had to rest. So in his time of rest the angel he trusted most, in whose hands he had placed all his faith, was jealous. And that angel persuaded others to act together with him against the will of God. And then God expelled those people from Heaven* and they came down from there. The first one to come down was the devil, the others are the spirits, the spirits who weren't content to leave Heaven and who came to earth to do evil, to enter your body to practice evil . . .

TWO

**DECIMATE**—to kill one in ten, Zoë thinks to herself. The word won't do. Is there a word for killing five or six in ten? *Demicide?* Half-extinguish? Can familiar combinations of vowels and consonants describe what has happened to Aparecida's generation in just a fraction of a generation? João Defunto—Dead-man John—is more than a nickname; now he's six feet under, and so are Cheira, Cristiano, Alejado, Véio, Manoel, Caveira, Bochecha, Loucura, Neguinho do Oião, Neguinho Sapato de Sola, Cara de Ovelha, and João Babão. Branca lost her head—severed at the neck (how much rage was needed to guide the knife?). Zé da Silva was hunted down by the drug traffickers he crossed, Ronaldo was run over by a bus. Gabione took his own life.

So perhaps with a name that means life, she is a walking misnomer. She is more a reluctant archivist of the dead, a collector of fleeting reminders that childhood can be an all-encompassing beginning, middle, end. She guesses she has the only remains of their voices, the last photographs: should I give these things to the mothers?

Half extinguished, that leaves one half still smoldering. The *demi-vivos?* Charles carrying his colostomy in a bottle at the waist; Margarete, with insanity her last shelter; Fia losing babies to the social workers and the police; Caco, Manoel, and Bira behind bars for crushing the skull of a schoolboy who refused to surrender his watch; Fábio no longer a street child, a homeless man but on the same corner and in the same stupor.

The last time Zoë had been in Recife, Latin American street children were the object of international scrutiny: media attention abounded, human rights campaigns were launched, and national leaders in Brazil, Colombia, Guatemala, and beyond found them-

selves having to account for the existence of death squads special-
ized in the murder of youths. Yet that attention ultimately proved
nearly as fleeting as the lives of the very homeless children that
advocates sought to protect. In retrospect, it occurs to Zoë, it is clear
that public understanding of violence against street children was
based on something like journalistic snapshots of particular children at particular (almost invariably tragic) moments or on accounts
by institutions seeking to raise money in the name of their young
charges. But there is something about this attention that makes it
unsustainable. The genocide in Rwanda, the Holocaust, the savagery
of Pol Pot, rape, torture, imprisonment, combat: all of these things
have a beginning, middle, and end, even if they reverberate indefi-
nitely in the lives of those who suffered the indignities or lost people
they loved. Events can be told as stories. But what if violence is not
so much an event as one of the few constant features in a person's
life? How does one frame that violence—not the violent death but
the violent life?

During the months of July, August, September, on till the end of
a particularly violent year, Aparecida and Zoë continue to meet in
the park, record their conversations, watch the passersby, fill cas-
settes, reminisce the dead. Zoë gives Aparecida a tape recorder of
her own, which she talks to at night. Sometimes she records her
conversations with others.

Fragments, vignettes, omissions, wishful thinking, incomplete
sentences, incoherencies, truths, deceits, hallucinations, oblivion.
*A cigarette? Have you got a cigarette?* (Is vice a luxury or merely an
affirmation of life?) *I'll be twenty-two in October. I can hardly believe
it.* But her disbelief is not at how fast time passes, it is that she
has lived to what strikes her as an improbably advanced age. Are
these the ingredients of a life story? Zoë, the archivist, Aparecida
admiring the reflected image of a riverine city, a city like a mother
impassive at the fate of her own battered child.

Looking at the growing cache of tapes and field notes, she remembers the tale of the Guatemalan Indian holed up for eight days in a
Paris apartment, recounting to the anthropologist the customs of
her people, the deaths of friends and family, the cruelty of a succes-

sion of dictatorships, the grief of searching for bones that cannot be found. Rigoberta Menchú eventually won the Nobel prize for peace but the royalties from the book went to the ethnographer who, curiously, otherwise wrote herself out of the text, omitting even her questions. Then another anthropologist entertained himself for a decade investigating and challenging the claims of the book. Inconsistencies? Or was it perhaps a case of the putative ingénue reading the imagined readership? How many of us, in any case, could tell our own lives in a way that would withstand such scrutiny?

This life, Aparecida's, it strikes Zoë, can only be told in the language she speaks: fragments, contradictions, regrets, stifled yearnings, deceptions, omissions, words laboriously drawn on the page. A life like the mouth of the Capibaribe: a current flowing from one place to another, to be sure, but subject to the tides, the mixture of fresh and salt water, the sordid runoff from the city, a meeting place spanned by decaying bridges. And so, like Aparecida who crochets into the night, Zoë begins to  knit together the incongruous strands, searching for the beginning in the middle, the denouement where it doesn't exist, translating, rephrasing, reinventing, bearing.

*When my mother's sperm mixed with my father's, my mother's was stronger. That's why my voice is not very deep, why I hardly have hair on my body when the hair on my head is thick and long.*

*At first we didn't live on the earth. We lived in the air, above the water. It was a place called Mangabeira, on the banks of the Capibaribe. A house on stilts, the water below us, the tides rising, falling, piss pattering ribbons between the cracks of the odd-sized planks and joining the river below, as if the river were the fluid where babies nestle. The river below but the river that would swell, rise with the full moon, and then we were no longer in the air, but in the water, swimming, swimming after plates and cups, plastic dolls, scraps of clothing, my mother in the water clinging to a piece of wood, the firemen coming to pull us out, to stop us from being swept away.*

*It was a little house and there were a lot of us to fit in there — my mother, seu Reginaldo, who was my stepfather, my brothers and sisters, myself. For a while my aunt came with her three children. Her husband had kicked them out of the house when he found a new woman. If there was a chicken to eat, we would all stand around the table, which had only three legs, and nibble from one another's plates. If you weren't watching, someone would take the food off your plate and put it in a pocket to eat it later.*

*Sometimes neighbors would come by and leave some food for us. They knew we had nothing. But then seu Reginaldo would come home and say, "Who left us this food? Today they give, tomorrow they'll come to collect!"*

*Sometimes women would come to my mother and say, "Maria, you might think I don't like you because I don't share any food with you. But it isn't that. It's because your husband doesn't like it." Other times, women would wait until seu Reginaldo had left the house, and then come by to leave something.*

*There was a woman who would buy carrots from me. Sometimes I would go to the market and steal carrots and then I would come back and sell them. She wanted to buy some carrots and some other vegetables that I had but she didn't have any money. Her husband didn't trust her with money. He would only give her exactly what he thought she needed. She wanted to buy the vegetables on credit. I said that would be all right. Then she told me, "My husband just brought home a lot of rice, beans, pasta, oil, and flour. I'm going to set some aside for you."*

*When seu Reginaldo came home and saw the bag of food, he waited for everyone to go to sleep. Then he went out and exchanged the food for drink. But the drink only made him hungrier and angrier. So he woke up everyone in the house. He was yelling and throwing things. He said that someone had stolen all the food that he had worked so hard to buy. That time he pretended he had been the one who brought home the food.*

*When we got up in the morning, there was no food and the radio was smashed. Even my mother's rocking chair was in pieces.*

*Take a stick and you can fish things out of the river: empty bottles, the left arm of a doll, plastic bags, decaying branches, drowned rats, their bellies inflated with water. You find toys everywhere there are children.*

*Like crabs emerging from deep tunnels, spreading every which way after something to eat, they would climb the hills, descend upon the river- banks, visit the houses of the poor. The politicians. They can always be seen before elections. They roll up their sleeves, remove their ties, shake hands. Roberto Freire, Gustavo Krause, Marco Maciel, they all came to Mangabeira. Some of them even visited our house, had something to eat—nervously, because they were afraid of our food. They talked about what they would do for us: a job for my mother, a better roof, clothing. Now, when I am sitting along the Rua da Aurora, watching the day go by, I see some of them walking into the Legislative Assembly. But I don't think they recognize me.*

*One day the politicians came to offer us something bigger than a job, something better than a basket of food or a bottle of medicine and more important than a lot of toys. We would no longer need to live in the air. We would live in the forest, outside the city. In a house not of wood and cardboard, plastic sheeting, stolen billboards, tin and tree branches. A* house made of bricks. The neighbors began to leave, all of their belongings loaded onto a small truck. One truck for each household. The politicians knew we couldn't hire men to move our things. We were the last family to leave. As our belongings were being placed in the back of the vehicle, the men were already preparing to burn the houses. A little gasoline, a match.

So when we no longer lived in the air, we lived in the forest, a place called Bola na Rede. At first there was no electricity there. Our only light was from candles and from the moon. Water, when it came, arrived by truck. There were no buses to take us into the city. Living in the forest, we didn't have to worry about waking up in the water, but the forest was a place of snakes. The neighbors put their beds on stilts, so the snakes couldn't come for them at night. We had only one bed. I slept on the floor, on the floor but with a stick in one hand.

When there was no food at home, I would go to the market. At first I went with my mother, then I went alone or with Marquinho, my neighbor. At first I just picked up pieces of old fruit, vegetables from the ground to take home or else I offered to carry things from one place to another in exchange for some fruit. But after a while I learned I could make money another way, by going off into the forest with men, kissing them, touching them. I would do that and then I would have some money to take home. I could buy rice or flour or oil, things we needed. I was six, then I was seven. Some time passed, and by then I was eight.

Each time I observed myself in the mirror I thought I looked a lot like one of my sisters. We were always similar, not only in appearance, but also in height. And so I looked at my face and it seemed to me that I had beautiful cheekbones, a nice throat. I wanted to run some lipstick across my lips, which were thick, full. When I looked in the mirror I saw a girl. Alone one day, I put on my sister's clothing.

Seu Reginaldo wasn't blind and he could see the effects of my mother's sperm. He would see me playing with girls, watch the way I walked. He observed me. Watched and observed. Sometimes, just to fool him, I would bring home a toy soldier, a little plastic man with a gun, and play with it on the floor. Other times I would kick a dog or throw stones at birds, do things that boys did, even though I didn't want to.

But still, there was a day when I was at home, looking after my younger siblings. He arrived drunk and I told him not to make so much noise. He told me to heat up some food. He was hungry.

I did what he told me. I heated up the food and filled his plate. Again I asked him not to make noise. I had just put the children to bed. Neguinha, Dara, Camila, Paulinho, they were asleep on their mattress and I was awake.

He didn't like what I had said, my tone of voice. He slapped me twice across the face. "The easy part is to have a child, the hard part is to raise it; your mother has spread her legs more times than Mary Magdalene, given birth more times than I can count, and where is she? She leaves me here to raise you, to teach you how to grow up."

I won't lie to you, I was afraid. When you are nine years old, you are afraid of men like that. He was drunk. No, it was more than that, he was possessed. Violence was with him, the spirit Violence.

The children were sleeping in the living room. I went to my room. When I thought I was sleeping, he opened the door and held one hand to my throat. With the other he threatened to cut me with a knife. Then he pried my mouth open and forced his way in. When he was done I thought he would go away, but he didn't. He tied my hands to the bedpost. I don't know how it ended because I fainted.

It was four o'clock when I woke up. I was bleeding. I went to take a bath and then it was five o'clock and the children were waking up, so I prepared their pap.

After seu Reginaldo was done and had fallen asleep and I was awake and making the pap for my brothers and sisters, my mother came home from work. She worked at night in a motel, cleaning. It was called O Cheiro do Amor, it doesn't exist any longer. A lot of other motels exist today, but not that one.

When I told my mother what had happened to me, she said I should go to the bathroom and wash myself. I told her I had already taken a bath, so she asked me to go out and buy bread. She gave me some money, but I didn't buy her anything. I walked to the highway and from there to the bus terminal. I went into the city.

They used to say there was a black car that would pick up children and steal their organs, their eyes, their heart, their lungs. Since I was always devoted to Nossa Senhora da Conceição, I asked the saint for protection. Because anyone can do anything to a child of that age.

I found an awning to sleep under. I slept, I dreamt dreams I will never be able to remember but that were probably about the grasping reach of vines, the twisting fibers that make a rope, the deaths of insects, and when it was the morning and I was still asleep, a lady came around. She shook me: "Are you hungry, child? Come with me."

I looked at her: a woman who wanted to know if I was hungry. I had always been a hungry child, so I followed her. She led me to a bakery and, without asking what I wanted, told the man to give us some sweet bread and a glass of guaraná. I ate the bread, sipped the drink. I felt the bubbles in my throat, in my stomach. I have never liked fizzy drinks, they remind me of my first house, of the one that was in the air, in the air with water all around.

Then the lady took me to a store and bought some clothing for me and asked me, "Do you want to live in my house?"

Live in her house? I thought for a moment. "No, I don't want to," I told her. "You might say you want to take me to your house but stop in the middle of the road and tear out my eyes."

"Child," she said, "are you mad? I want to help you. I want to show you that you have the chance to live a good life."

I stood there, motionless but wanting to run.

Her eyes were looking down and she saw that the new shorts she had just bought me were bloodied. She asked me what had happened.

"I fell."

**A LIFE IS NEVER RECOUNTED** in the way we want to hear it, Zoë knows, and so she had begun writing as she wanted the life to unfold, culling like the ragpicker from what is rejected, from the interruptions that separate the pauses, the first three words of a sentence on page eight of the transcriptions united with seven words from page four hundred and sixteen. But not precisely the same words, for they are translated, recast, reinvented. A translation without a certain original?

Where does this life begin? With an unremembered birth, with the act of rape, with flight to the street? Somewhere else within the amphetamine-strewn haze of violence, boredom, fear, revolt? To Zoë, it had seemed that Aparecida's life began when she herself found a boy drawing in a smoothed pile of dust, sand, and earth on the patio of a crumbling house. Though at first she had tried to know about his past, she had managed to discover almost nothing. In the absence of any knowledge of what he had lived before that time, she came to feel that he had no past. He was who he was when she discovered him, though she might have been able to make him into something else. Aparecida was steeped in a pain that could be found at almost any juncture in her life and that extended in many directions. Which memories are oldest? Aparecida says she remembers and Zoë re-members, takes the pieces as she finds them, joins one with another.

*I didn't know if the city was dangerous, if other children were going to hurt me. At that time, I had no experience. That is what the street gives you, experience.*

The other children didn't hurt me. They came to be like my family. They were my brothers and sisters, my father, my mother. There is the family that the accident of fate gives you and there is the family that we make for ourselves. I found mine here, at night, on the bridges, along the docks, under awnings, clinging with me to the backs of buses. Sometimes we would fight, like when the spiritists came to bring us food and someone would cut in line. So we would start arguing, yelling at one another, pushing, cursing, and before you knew it, we were friends. When I stopped and looked around me, I saw that I wasn't the only child living in the street.

I met Safira. She was ten and I was nine. She's always one year older than I am. She had a lot more experience in the street than I did and the children respected her. So I got together with her and her band: Paula, Galega, Miúda, Fia, Liliane, Jeane, Cherosa, Menininha. They were all girls, except for me.

I got together with them and we went to take what belonged to other people. One day, I was with three girls on Conde da Boa Vista and one of them took a woman's bag. The woman was pregnant and fell to the ground. She was so afraid that her waters broke. The sidewalk was wet, the three girls ran, I ran too, but when I saw the woman on the sidewalk, a crowd gathering around her, I turned and walked back. I felt bad for her, so bad that I said I had been the one who robbed her. When the police came, they hit me. The woman was conscious again, and she said I hadn't been the one. Other people agreed, but it didn't make any difference. The police said the woman was protecting me because she was afraid. All along I knew that if she had lost the child, one way or another I was going to have to pay, and I preferred to pay in this life.

I made a promise to Nossa Senhora da Conceição, and it was as if she heard me, because since then I haven't wanted to take things from people. I've seen a lot of street children beaten up, it doesn't matter that they're minors. You can be beaten to a pulp for stealing a necklace. Once, I was hit and for months, blood and pus dripped from my ear.

To earn my money more honestly, I touched men in the way they wanted to be touched. I thought that if I earned money honestly that it would last longer, that I could buy the things I needed and I wouldn't have to worry if I went up to a street vendor or into a store to buy some clothing, that someone might say I was spending stolen money. Even if

*they were going to insult me because the money was from prostitution,
it was money earned honestly. I wasn't taking anything that belonged to
anyone else.*

*I would go out with men, but there was no penetration. I was only
ten. I would touch them and they would give me some spare change, a
handout, some food, one thing or another. It was also a matter of getting
experience, I wanted to learn. At the time I was very young, I had never
gotten into a car with a strange man. But the men who paid me to go out
with them thought only about feeling pleasure. It didn't matter to them
that I was a child.*

*At the time there was a transvestite who was very successful, Roberta
Close. So I went to my mother, one day when I was visiting her at home,
and asked her, "Mother, if some day I were to become a transvestite like
Roberta Close, would you allow me in the house?" And she said, "You
will always be my son."*

*But things did not turn out the way I wanted them to. When I went
back home that time, it was about New Year's and one year was becoming
another. My mother embraced me. It had been a long time since she had
last seen me. But when seu Reginaldo saw me, he pulled my hair, slapped
my face, ripped my clothing, the clothing that covered my body but that I
had bought by uncovering my body. It was the same kind of money I had
used to buy presents for my family. I ran. I had no way to defend myself: a
child, a man. I ran back to the center of Recife and went on with my life.*

*And in my life, I met a woman, a journalist. She was researching
something else, but you know how reporters are, they see a story and they
pursue it, to make themselves some money. She saw me in the street. I was
only twelve but I had long hair. I dressed like a woman. I was wearing a
short skirt and a tight blouse. She stopped me and offered me a snack. She
wanted to know how old I was when I left home. Why I had left. So I told
her I had left at the age of nine, because my stepfather raped me.*

*Then seu Reginaldo hated me even more, because he came to be known
as a rapist. His relatives saw me on the news and they didn't have a
good impression of him. When the relatives of my stepfather have a bad
impression of someone, they want to kill him.*

*So I had to roam somewhere else. That was when I went to Casa
Caiada, in Olinda. I not only went to another place, I disguised myself as*

a boy. It had been a while since I had been a boy, I had almost forgotten what it meant. I found myself shorts and T-shirts. That wasn't difficult. The hard part was walking like a boy and speaking like one, and pretending that I liked video games and throwing rocks. Those things didn't come naturally to me. But for a time I was among people who hadn't known me as a girl and who didn't know I was only pretending to be a boy like any other.

I slept in abandoned cars and under awnings and fed myself by making friends with the waiters at restaurants, so they would give me leftover food. There were a lot of nice ladies in that neighborhood and some of them would give me breakfast in the morning. But when I had nothing to eat, nothing at all, I would be tempted to look through the trash for food. It's something that dogs do and I was always observing the dogs because I found them nicer than people, nicer at least than men. And I thought to myself, if dogs will never do harm because it gives them pleasure and they eat from the trash, why am I better than them? Why can't I bring myself to do the same? One day it was a holiday and everything was closed. The shops were shuttered and people were sleeping in their houses or they had gone away to the beach. That was when I saw a sandwich half eaten in the trash, it was one of those blue plastic trash cans that hang from the light poles. I looked at what was left of the sandwich and it invited me to pick it up, hold it, bite into it. It had cheese and ham and mayonnaise and it tasted good, even though it was a little dry. I finished it and then I wasn't so hungry. But a few hours later it was as if I had a fierce animal in my stomach, clawing at my insides, biting.

When I woke up I was in the hospital. I thought I had died but I had only been sick. It was as if my stepfather and all his relatives had placed the sandwich in the bin to tempt me. We can rape you and we can tempt you, they were saying. We can tear you apart from inside.

I liked to draw. I still do. It is a gift I have. I never tried to learn. I just applied my finger to the sand or cut my wrists to get a little blood and I was drawing. I draw what comes to me, and almost always it is goddesses and women I've never seen in life. So I was drawing one woman when another came to me. A real woman. She spoke a strange language I'd never heard before. She spoke with our words but at the same time every word was different. Her tongue worked differently from the way ours does. So even though she didn't speak our language, I understood her. She was as pale as the women on television.

She asked me what I was drawing and then she asked me a lot of other questions. She wanted to know how old I was and where I had learned to draw, who my parents were and where I lived. What does this woman really want? I wondered. What place is she from and what do people wish for in that place? When you don't know who you are or where you came from or what you are doing here, it is best to be a person dreamed up by someone else. Then if there is something wrong with you, it isn't your doing.

Not only did she speak a strange tongue, but like the figures I would draw she seemed more a creation of my imagination than something born here or there, just like that. I wanted to know why her toenails were unpainted, what she carried in her bag, where she came from and what it was like and if it was a place I would like to go one day. I wanted to know what she ate and whether she dreamed in her tongue or in ours and how she had gotten here. I thought that if I listened carefully that I would learn the answers to these questions.

She would visit me in the street and I wanted to know why. Other people would stop and talk with us, but they were the people who were in the street anyway, Zé Maluco, the locksmith, Maria Gordinha, who sells flowers, seu Kleber, the owner of the lumber yard. There were lots of people who spoke with street children. But this woman was different. She went to the street because she wanted to find me. Why? That is what I had to find out. Did she want to sell my organs? Did she want to undress in front of a child?

One day she invited me to her apartment. I had never been in a tall building before, and I had always thought it would be difficult to climb to the top of one. I didn't know how fat people or old people could make it all the way up. Seu Geraldo, the doorman at her building, knew me and when he saw me entering the front gate with the woman he looked at me as if to say, "You shouldn't be here." Or was he saying, "Be careful"?

We climbed the building by entering a tiny room. More than a room, it was like an upright coffin. The doors closed and I thought, what a strange place she has taken me to. Then all of a sudden, my entrails fell to the floor and the rest of me was rushing toward the ceiling, only no part of me, so far as I could see, was moving. We were in an elevator but at the time I didn't even know the word.

She lived in a big apartment that was almost empty. From what I had seen looking through ground-floor windows, most people want to fill their emptiness with a lot of furniture. I prefer the emptiness because it is precisely what's missing in the street. That is when I began to trust her a little. She was comfortable with emptiness.

She had a terrace. Standing on the terrace made my head spin and my feet felt like they had nothing beneath them. The highest I had ever been was up a tree. Being in the high branches of a tree can make you wonder how you'll get down again, but this was different. I had climbed trees before but I had never looked down on a coconut tree from the top. It was like being on the ground and looking up a ladies skirt. It was something you didn't do. In that sense, everything was backwards. And then there was the sea. Looking at the sea from up high means you see further because the earth is the shape of an egg and from up there you can almost see around to the other side. But whatever is on the other side must be very small, because there was no sign of it.

"Why are you here?" I asked her one day. She looked at me and thought for a moment and said, "I don't know . . . my parents made me."

I liked her answer but it wasn't really the answer to the question I had been thinking. "Why did you come to Pernambuco?" I said.

"I am a student. I am studying the culture of street children. What they say about their lives, what they do, how they survive, the games they play, things like that."

"You're a journalist."

"Journalists are like flies," she said. "They see something appetizing, they feed for a moment, and then they go away. We stay for a long time. To try to see how things really work."

"You're like a bicho-do-pé" then? I asked.

"A bicho-do-pé?"

"Those little bugs that burrow into your foot and stay for a long time?"

I liked to walk around her empty house. The floors were ceramic and they were cold on my feet. I liked touching cold things. She had a refrigerator.

*Even though I had seen a lot of refrigerators, I had never put my head inside one and felt the cold. Where she came from, the air was like that sometimes, she told me.*

*She would look at me in a strange way, as if she were longing for something. Most people long for money or sex, but in her case it was something else. She wouldn't tell me what it was. It was just a look she had. There was something she wanted, something she didn't have. She wouldn't say what it was but, even so, for a while, I wanted to be that something.*

I went back into the city and that's how it was. No one could stop me, not God, not my mother, not the woman who fed me and clothed me and tried to know my thoughts by watching me with her slow eyes. It wasn't just that the center of the city had a way of pulling me back, saying that my soul belonged to it. Nor was it just that enough time had gone by for seu Reginaldo to have forgotten about me, which might have been the case. It was that I had been a boy long enough. I wanted to be a girl again. Even more, I wanted to be a woman. I started wearing skirts and high heels and blouses again. I let my nails grow and bought nail polish. I stopped cutting my hair and bought a special brush. Every woman has breasts and at the very least, I wanted breasts. So I went to talk with other transvestites, to find out what they did: "Ei, bicha! Why is your skin so smooth? Why are your hips so full?" They told me about contraceptive pills. In women, the pills prevent them from having children; in us, they make us more womanly. They make our voices higher, our skin smoother, our hips rounder, they give us breasts, little ones, like small oranges. They can even make us feel jealousy the way women feel jealousy.

The only way we have of changing our bodies without feeling pain is by taking contraceptives, which are meant for women. If we take contraceptives, we don't feel any pain at all but we run the risk of getting a tumor in the stomach. Anyone who takes pills runs that risk. But if a fairy appeared to me and said, "Aparecida, if you would like, I can change your body," I would allow myself to dream a little. I would tell the fairy that I want the eyes of Bruna Lombardi, the hair and nose of Lúcia Veríssimo, the mouth and body of Isadora Ribeiro.

In the street, I would see children who were only seven or eight years old walking around with notebooks, writing more or less well. I looked at them and I said, my God, I don't even know how to hold a pen. I have to learn, at least how to write my own name. So I was roaming all over

the city and as you know, there are a lot of advertisements in Recife, it's
a city of propaganda. So I would walk around and look at those signs
and memorize the letters until I knew all of them. I still didn't know how
to put them together and write a word, but I could recognize all of them.
As I would pass by I would see those signs that indicate the names of
shops, of streets, and after a while there wasn't a sign in the city I hadn't
read. I learned how to read before I could even write. Whenever I see
a newspaper, a magazine, an old book in the garbage, I pick it up and
start reading. Sometimes I find really interesting things. Once I found
a book called Cristiane F. Later I sold the book, but I read it first. It's
about a thirteen-year-old girl, in Germany, a rich girl, but she wasn't
accepted by her parents because she hung out with foreigners and hippies
and people like that. So she decided to leave home. She got mixed up in
the world of crime and drugs, she sold her body, she had to kill in order to
buy drugs.

Once, I found a pamphlet that talked about a woman who was as rich
as she was evil, but she found herself in a terrible situation. She lost her
health and she was hospitalized. She spent all of her money looking for
a cure for her problem, but she didn't find one. So there she was, spending everything she had in life for a little health and I was destroying the
health that I had. So for a while I stopped using drugs.

There was a day when my mother came to look for me in the street, to
take me home again. But she was still suspicious because she didn't believe what I had told her about seu Reginaldo. I told her that I liked a boy
named George who went to school and lived near where we lived, and that
I didn't like girls. She understood all that but she said to me, "If you don't
want trouble with your stepfather, bring a girl to the house and say that
she is your girlfriend." At the time, the only one who understood me was
a girl named Rosa. She was eleven. She liked girls and I liked boys, so we
understood one another. I came home and I said, "Mother, this is Rosa.
She is my girlfriend." We even exchanged kisses in front of my mother.
But everyone knew it was just a role I had assumed. When I took some
money and went to buy vegetables, people would still taunt me. So George
stayed where he was and Rosa too, and I went back to the city.

*Those scars on my arms are the result of the things that have happened
to me. At first, I noticed that the girls in the street did those things to
themselves, cut their arms. Jeane, Margarete, Menininha, they all had
those scars. I thought that maybe it was something that identified the girls
as belonging to the group. But then I saw that each girl had a different
reason for having scars. Sometimes when the police would come to take
away their bottle of glue, to hit them, to arrest them, the girls would pick
up a piece of glass and cut themselves, threaten to smear the policemen's
uniforms with blood. But in my case it was different. I would only cut my
arms when I missed things I had never known. One day I cut the vein
that runs from my wrist to my heart. A policeman found me in the street
and took me to the hospital. The nurses sewed me up. Six days later, I cut
myself again.*

*Mother's Day was one of the times when I missed my family most.
I had no one to sit down with, to talk with. I would see other children
giving gifts to their mothers, mothers hugging their children, thanking
their children. So it was pain I felt, and this was the only way I could find
to ease it: I would take a piece of glass, cut my arm, and watch the blood
trickle down. When the blood stopped dripping, I would look at it, sniff
some more glue, and make shapes and figures in the blood. That is how I
started drawing—wetting the tip of my index finger, forming images on
the sidewalk.*

*Other times I would buy a shirt, some flowers, and go up to an old
homeless lady in the street and give her those things. There are a lot of old
ladies in the street. Some of them are alcoholics, some of them have been
abandoned by their children. There are impatient children, you know,
children who kick their grandmother or mother out of the house. Some
of them are running out of steam, expiring. So for me, it would be like
having a mother, not my real one, not the one who put me in the world,
but a mother, someone I could give something to. I never had the respect
of society, of rich people, the ones who helped me the most were the poor,
the desperate ones.*

*There was a woman named Dona Penha who would sleep outside the
Igreja do Carmo. I went there one night to sleep and I gave my bag to her
and asked if she would watch over it while I slept. She took it and watched
over it. This is what I was thinking, being at her side. She was a woman*

I had never seen before but there was something in her that made me feel better. I knew that at home, my mother, seu Reginaldo, my brothers and sisters, they may not have been thinking about how I was in the street, if I had a safe place to sleep, if I had enough to eat, whether or not I was sick. But I would wonder how they were, whether they had enough to eat. From then on, every time I would be with Dona Penha, I would feel comforted. I felt happy at her side, as if she had been my grandmother or my mother in a past life. She accepted me. She would give me advice, tell me to give up sniffing glue. So it was as if she taught me manners, because at the time I was ignorant.

When I was in the street and people would walk by, they would look at me as if I were an animal, a dog, nothing at all. People would look at me and I would think, what are they looking at? Have they never seen a faggot, a transvestite? And sometimes I would get so angry I would throw stones. I had been humiliated so many times by so many people, I thought everyone was the same, that they all had the same capacity to hate. But Dona Penha taught me that that wasn't quite right. If everyone were the same, they would have been made on an assembly line.

"Don't cry, put your head here. Your mother is fine," she would tell me. And when I put my head in her lap the tears fell even faster. Sometimes the tears would loosen the dirt on my face.

*We are taking a chance, we do it because we are hungry.
It is a risk to get inside the car of a man we don't know.
He takes you to a motel, you do what you have to do,
then he points a gun in your face, tells you to get out of
the car. The bitch that brought us into this world . . .
It is our feminine side they take advantage of.*

*And twenty-four hours a day, I was walking around
in the middle of the street dressing like a girl. Sometimes
photographers would stop me and take my picture and
then I would appear in the* Jornal do Commércio *or
in the* Diário de Pernambuco. *At first I thought it was
because I was sniffing glue but then I realized that it was because I was so
young and dressed up like a woman. Once I found a newspaper in the garbage, with my face in a photograph. It said, "The Youngest Transvestite
in Recife Comes Out of the Closet."*

*Another time, though, a woman stopped me in the street. I was wear-
ing some heels that were about this high* (an index finger and thumb
splayed opposite directions) *and a skirt that didn't reach my knees. The
woman wasn't a journalist. She asked, "How long have you been dressing
like that?"*

*"Since I was nine."*

*"Look," she said, "your skirt is perfect, so is your blouse. The only thing
that doesn't work are the shoes, walking around in heels like that during the day. Women don't wear that sort of heel during the day. I'm not
trying to criticize you, it's just that I think you should observe us a little
more carefully."*

*So I took that as good advice and tried to watch women more carefully.*

*And she said, "Your cheeks are very nice, and your neck. If you apply
your eyeliner more carefully, you'll look just like Greta Garbo."*

*I was happy because instead of reproaching me for wanting to be like
a woman, she was encouraging me, giving me advice. Now I look for my
own reflection more in women than in the mirror.*

*One day a friend named José Maria came up to me and said, "Aparecida,
Bertrán wants to talk with you." Bertrán was a man who had a group for
street children. He was from a family with a house and a car and a telephone, but he had come to live in the street for a while, as an adolescent.
Some people said he liked to have sex with the street children but I didn't
believe that.*

*"About what?"*

*"About a movie he wants to make."*

*"A movie?"*

*"Yes, a movie, and he wants you to be in it."*

*So I went to find out what all this talk about a movie meant. Bertrán
wanted to make a movie, so he could go to Spain and Italy and São Paulo
and other places to show it and make money for his group.*

*"It's the only way I can help you," Bertrán said.*

*I didn't think Bertrán could help me at all, but at the same time I
wanted to be in a movie. It's another way of being who you aren't, and I
had never tried that way.*

*At the time I was working in the flower market, selling flowers for Dona
Inês. I helped her arrange flowers for funerals. So I said, "Bertrán, I'll
have to speak to my boss, Dona Inês, to see if she gives me permission.
And you have to know that if I'm going to be in your movie, I'm missing
out on my job."*

*He had me do a lot of things, like walk across the Iron Bridge dressed
in nothing but my underwear, walk along the edge of the river, talk about
homosexuality and prostitution. He had other people, like Chefe, shoot
up. One of the boys who shot up with Chefe lost his arm. Now he can't
work because his arm doesn't exist any more.*

*When I finished doing what I had to do for that movie, I went back
to Dona Inês, but she had given my job to someone else. So I didn't
have work; Bertrán gave me a* cesta básica: *rice, beans, toilet paper, oil,
salt . . . I took the basket home to my mother, but that was all I got for
the film.*

*The movie was shown here in the Teatro do Parque and a lot of people went to see it and they all told me that my performance was the best part of the whole show. Then Bertrán went to the other world, to Italy, and when he came back he had a car, an office, telephones, an apartment, a whole lot of things.*

*For a time, my place was outside the Casa da Cultura. That was where
I would wait for clients, and that is where I met Andréa, a dark-skinned
transvestite who traveled a lot.*

*She came up to me and said, "Bicha, you are nice, you are pretty,
but you need to think about your future: you have to get yourself a little
money. Listen to me, you don't want to be an old transvestite wandering
around the streets of Recife with a bottle of glue in one hand and people
laughing at you. Come with me, we'll travel."*

*So I stopped and I looked at her and I thought about her words and
it seemed to me that there was a certain truth to them. Then she said,
"Come on, let's travel to Salvador."*

*I'd never been to Salvador. In fact, I'd never been anywhere. As far as
I knew, the whole world was Recife, Olinda, the mangrove swamps, the
forest outside the city. I went to get my clothing, which was in the house
of a woman on the Rua Velha, in the neighborhood of Boa Vista. Then I
came back to meet Andréa outside the train station. We got on the train
and got off at the highway. Once we were there, we had to wait for a day
and a half to get a ride. It was on the second day that someone stopped. I
didn't have any experience talking to people in trucks so I said to Andréa,
"Andréa, you get in first." But the man didn't like that, he wanted me to
sit next to him. So I climbed up and I asked the man where he was going
and he said he was going to the state of Bahia. I asked if he could take us
with him and he said he could.*

*Each time the man put his hand on the gearshift he would touch my leg
and laugh. So I said, "Sir, are you giving me this ride with the hope that
along the way I will do something for you?"*

*"No," he said, "I'm giving you a ride. If something else happens, you'll
get whatever you are owed."*

*So I said all right.*

*We continued traveling and when it was late he stopped because he was tired and he was afraid of falling asleep while driving. Andréa slept in the front and the man and I went in the back where there were two miniature beds. He did what he had to do with me. He did it for three days and in the end, when we were in Bahia, he paid me. He gave me money and he also gave me a gold necklace with the image of Nosso Senhor do Bomfim. Giving me the necklace was the best thing he did for me.*

*Andréa and I got off at the square and walked to the Lacerda Elevator. I thought it was a chance to ride another elevator. But when we arrived, she said to me, "Aparecida, wait here with your bag. I'm going to take mine to a bar so they can watch it for me, then I'll come back and get you."*

*We had arrived in Salvador at eleven o'clock and after a while it was noon, then one o'clock, then two thirty. Later it was seven. So I was alone in Salvador where I didn't know a soul. I didn't know what you needed to do to survive in that city, what people in Salvador were like, if they were the same as in Recife or if they were different. I was missing Recife and started to cry. And as I was crying a young woman, who was a prostitute, felt sorry for me. She asked me where I was from and I told her that I was from Recife. She said, "I could tell you're from Recife, because of the way you speak. Do you have money?"*

*I said I had twenty-five cruzeiros. I didn't show her the necklace.*

*She said that with twenty-five cruzeiros, I could only spend six days in that city, because I'd have to pay three and a half cruzeiros per day for a room, not counting food.*

*The owner of the boardinghouse where she took me was called Rosa do Facão, Rosa with the Big Knife, because anytime a client was stirring up trouble with one of the transvestites, she would pull out her big knife and go downstairs to see what was happening.*

*Rosa with the Big Knife saw how she could give me money and tell me to go out and buy bread. And I would bring her the bread and the change. If I saw that the bathroom was dirty, I would clean it. At the end of the six days I showed her the gold necklace. She said, "Aparecida, you can stay here for a year without paying anything. When I need something, you will serve me. Just give me that necklace and you'll have a place to sleep and food to eat."*

*After a while, when I got to know the other transvestites, I went down to* the Avenue to fazer a vida, *which is what we call it, to make life. I made a lot of enemies in that life. I wouldn't get into the cars, I would just stand outside and show my face, my breasts, my behind. The men would stay in their cars, watching me. But the other transvestites wanted me to get in the cars like they did, take the keys and then, with their help, rob the client . . . They wanted me to do that but I wouldn't, so they were angry with me.*

*There was a transvestite named Caricata, whose face was scarred from an accident and who had no idea how to apply make-up. She was ugly and bald. One night I had turned three tricks and made myself some money and I had even been given a special box. It had two swans and in the middle a little ballet dancer that spun around when you opened the lid. That was when Caricata came and took my money.*

*So I said, "All right. This is the first time. This time you took my money, but if you do it again, it isn't going to work out for you." I said that even though she was older and taller than I was. She hit me, so I hit her back. I bit her breasts and grabbed her wig and threw it in the gutter. She picked up a broken bottle and slashed my face, which is why I have this scar here. When I saw my blood, I ran away.*

*Four days later, she came with three other transvestites who grabbed me and held me down. I had very long hair at the time, down to my waist; Caricata took a pair of scissors and cut it all off.*

*I went back to the boardinghouse, crying, and Rosa with the Big Knife took care of me. She wanted me to defend myself. After four days she gave me a wig — my hair was so short — and she said, "Aparecida, you can go down and do life again. Just take this little bottle with you."*

*It was a deodorant bottle, Avanço, but inside was a solution of muriatic acid. "Throw this at Caricata's face. If you don't, when you come back here, I'll rearrange the part of your face that wasn't cut." Then she started laughing. She had big teeth, the kind that can bite through a chicken bone.*

*I ran off to the room of a transvestite named Surama to ask if Rosa with the Big Knife would really do to me what she had threatened to do. Surama said, "Boneca . . . Doll, don't worry. She's just trying to make you feel better. But if you want to know what I think, I think you should do it. That way Caricata won't be able to boss you around."*

So if it was for my own good, then I should do it. That's what I was thinking. At the same time, my heart was beating very fast and the idea came to me that maybe it shouldn't be so hard to forgive Caricata? God was able to forgive the worst sinners in the world, so why shouldn't I be able to forgive Caricata?

But then I thought, I'm not God.

So I went down to the avenue and turned my first trick, then my second. I turned four tricks that night and put the money inside one of the boots I was wearing. Caricata saw all that and her eyes grew with envy. She came over and told me to take off my boot and give her the money. I did that and she went to have a drink in a bar.

I stood there on the corner. When she saw me, on the other side of the street, she called out to me and said, "Give me a cigarette." So I went over and gave her a cigarette. Then she said, "Give me a light." She was insulting me, saying terrible things. I opened my bag but instead of pulling out my lighter, I pulled out the bottle of deodorant. I threw the acid at her face and it dripped down on her chest and her legs. Her face was burning, she was melting, smoke rose from her cheeks.

I had never seen anything like that. I was afraid.

She screamed from pain. I ran. I ran and ran and ran and when I reached Lacerda, a policeman saw me running and he ran after me. He ran faster than I could and he caught me.

He asked me why I was running and I told him that I had been running since the day I was born.

"Where were you born?"

"In Bahia."

"You don't speak like someone who was born here."

"That's funny," I said. "I was born right here."

He didn't believe me. "How old are you?"

"Fifteen," I said, which was true. I had been there for a year, which is why I was fifteen. He put me in his car and took me to FEBEM, where I was locked up with all the other lost and abandoned kids, and the criminals among them. One day I had an interview with a social worker. I was lucky because she was from Recife. She had been working in Bahia for a while, but she was from Recife. She went with me to the boardinghouse to

*get my things and she traveled with me back to Recife—the social worker
and two guards.*

*I stayed there for two months, in* FEBEM *in Recife, locked up and eating bread leavened by the devil, waiting to see if my mother would come.
There are guards at* FEBEM *who visit the girls at night. One of the guards
put me in a separate room and when I woke up at night he was rubbing
his member against my face.*

*In the end, no one came for me, so the first chance I had, I climbed over
the wall and ran away.*

*Outside, there were so many men that it was hard to feel love for any
of them. When I had money, I'd sleep in a boardinghouse, when I didn't,
I'd sleep in the street. That's why I never tried loving anyone. Love stirs
you up, from inside. If you give in to love, you are capable of doing anything in its name. And when you aren't loved in return, you can even kill.
The worst thing is to love and not be loved. So I try not to love anyone.
I admire, I contemplate, but that is different.*

*If you ask me, we know only the afternoon, where we are today, but no
one knows what will happen when night falls. At any moment we can be
set alight; there are people who would do that: throw gasoline on us, toss a
match. That is the risk we run. But life is the trees, the birds, all the things
of nature taken together. Without those things, where would we be? The
dogs, the cats, the night, the rats that sometimes crawl onto the cardboard
where we lay our heads. All of that is a form of life.*

As Zoë translates and composes this last paragraph, her mother
comes to mind. The words could have been Stella's.

Her mother had studied music. She taught violin, but she was also
an economist of sorts, an economist of the emotions. Nine years old
when forty-six thousand Jews were put on trains from Salonika and
sent to Poland. Five months in 1943, and Greece's holocaust was
more complete than that of any other country. Only five percent of
those deported from Salonika survived. But by that time Stella was
in Spain and had been there for more than a year. Her own mother,
the grandmother Zoë never met, had seen the writing on the wall,

writing that few others had recognized. Stella's two brothers and her father had remained in Greece, hoping to wait out the war. Waiting, in that case, proved a fatal error. And Stella's mother committed a fatal error of her own, she yearned for the family to be reunited.

"At the age of nine, I knew something my mother didn't," Stella had told Zoë. "There was no place for yearning. Life was difficult enough for the Spaniards after the civil war, hundreds of thousands of whom had fled for France, Mexico, Argentina . . . Spain was hardly a place where any rational soul would seek refuge. The only thing between us and starvation was one remove from feeling; a broken heart is worse than a collapsed artery. You know, you can worry only in relation to the future, to what will happen or to what we will discover has already taken place. The key is to forget the future."

As a child, Zoë had wondered how one can forget what has not yet occurred. Yet over time she had come to understand that her mother believed she had survived the war by not feeling, by not praying for it to end, by not expecting to find her father and brothers, by not waiting, by not playing, by not worrying, by not projecting herself into a future whose advent or inviability depended in any way on her own desires. And by not recalling what was better about an irrecoverable past, she gripped life and contained it within an unnourished body. Her grandmother's hope, that the Nazis would not invade Greece, that they would be defeated if they did, her waiting for word of Greek Jews returning to Salonika, for history not to happen, may have been something like an essential gesture. But whereas Stella's mother had survived the Holocaust, or at least evaded it, despair— which, if one goes to the heart of the word, is the condition of not waiting, of not hoping—proved as lethal as the gas, or the flames, or the bullets, or the hunger, or the elements themselves. There was never any news. None whatsoever.

Stella's mother fell from a station platform in the outskirts of Madrid, just as the train was arriving. But what sort of a fall was it? The platform was crowded and there was luggage and farm produce scattered about, countless things she might have tripped over. But is it possible she jumped? Or was she pushed by invisible hands, the sort that appear to people hounded by the disembodied chatter Zoë knows well? Zoë never had reason to doubt what her mother thought about that question.

So Stella, at the age of thirteen, had lost her mother, her father, her two brothers, and every relative she had ever met or heard of except for the aunt who had received her in Spain. Gone as well were her home, her city, and any motive for return. She retained only the ability to exist in the present. It would not be accurate to say she was saved by a will to live. Will implies a commitment to the future; her salvation was a proficiency at bearing the present.

In time, Stella, sixteen and in the company of her aunt, was on a boat bound for New York, the city that would be her home until Zoë returned a box of ashes to Salonika. To Salonika? A city her mother had never wanted to see again while alive? And why cremation? A Jew asking to be burned? Hadn't enough members of the family been burned already? But Zoë learned a lot of things in the wake of her mother's death, such as why she herself had been given a name in a language her mother had otherwise refused to speak. Stella hadn't thought up the name herself; it was her own mother's, the name of Zoë's grandmother. You will take up where my mother left off, Stella had once said.

*So after I had gone to live in the street I went home one day. It was the Day of the Child and I had stolen a lot of toys to bring home to my brothers and sisters. When I arrived, I knocked on the door. Seu Reginaldo opened up. I was very surprised because he didn't hit me or insult me.*

*"Where have you been?" he asked. "I was worried."*

*"I was in the city. Is there anything to eat here?"*

*"Coffee and bread."*

*"I wanted bread and eggs."*

*"Here, take this money and buy yourself two eggs."*

*I was surprised by his generosity. When the alms are too bountiful, the blind man mistrusts . . . I mistrusted but I went and bought two eggs, came back home and ate them with a piece of bread.*

When I had finished eating, I asked, "When is my mother coming home?"

"It looks to me like she'll only be home tomorrow morning. She went to visit her sister. Your aunt is ill."

I missed my mother a lot, so I decided to stay.

"Are you going to wait for your mother to come home and then return to the city?"

"No, I think this time I'm going to stay."

"That's a good idea. The street is no place for you."

I didn't believe the spirit of his words. I meant to stay up all night, to wait for my mother. I turned on the television. It was a black and white television. I was watching television and I began to get sleepy. At the time there was only one bed in the house, my mother's. So I put down a cushion on the floor in the living room, near the door, so that if I heard the slightest noise I could open up for my mother.

At a certain hour of the night I woke up and he had one hand over my mouth and the other around my throat. He carried me to the bed and tied me down.

When he was finished, I said, "Can you untie me? I have to go to the bathroom."

"You think a real woman is that frail?"

He untied me. I went outside to where the toilet is but I didn't use it. I climbed over the wall in the back yard and began to run, to run . . .

 When I am not running, walking is one of my favorite things. I like to be familiar with the streets, admire old houses. If I see an abandoned house, a big one built by slaves, I stop in front of it and think, "What family lived in this house?" I touch the wall. How old is this house? Often, when I reach a crossroads, I begin to feel someone is walking with me.

I had one real on me and my stomach was rumbling. I was walking in that state. I stopped to buy a piece of cake and a cup of coffee. I had ten cents left over. I bought a cigarette. Then I continued walking. I walked

along Visconde Suassuna, and when I arrived at the third crossroads,
I turned right on the Rua do Sossego.

The Rua do Sossego is a very calm street. All you see there are trees,
walls, bats in flight. I like to watch bats fly. With all of the streetlights
along the Rua do Sossego, it's easy to see where you are going. Sometimes,
when I walk, I like to look not in front of me but down at the ground.
When I am walking and looking down at the ground, I'm thinking. My
mind is a long way away, remembering something.

I came to a place where there was the electric sign of a clinic. A big
light with letters on it. I stood near it in front of a wall and looked at my
shadow, which was falling across a wall. I decided to fix my hair. But
when I looked for the shadow of myself on the wall, I saw another shadow,
a shadow that wasn't my own. The figure in the shadow had longer hair
than I did and was wearing a skirt, even though I was wearing pants.
At that very instant I dropped my bag. My glue, my comb, my yarn, my
sandals: everything fell this way or that. I screamed, I ran. I ran to the
police booth near the Lojas Americanas and told the officer what had
happened.

"There was a shadow, but it wasn't mine. When I turned around to
look, there was no one there who could have cast the shadow!"

And I would wander, wander around the Rua das Flores, around José
Araújo, the fabric store. I would go up to the first floor and watch the
seamstresses. I got to like those people and they got to like me. They made
me feel better. I would sit there, they would give me a sheet of paper,
Marilene, Ivani, Maria José—they were some of the seamstresses that
were there. One would give me a pencil, another one a sheet of paper, still
another an eraser, and I would sit there, off in a corner, drawing. So I
started learning with them. Then they were transferred to the José Araújo
in the shopping mall and I never heard from them again. That was the
time when I would hang out on the sidewalks outside the Lojas Pernam-
bucanas. It was around there where I met Arruda Júnior, who was also
very good to me. He was a famous designer who knew a lot about fashion.
He lived in Afogados and he liked me a lot and he took me home with
him, to live there. He was helping me get my papers sorted out, my birth

certificate, trying to get me enrolled in school. But I was too hardheaded, it was another chance I lost. I went into his house like a sardine and came out as fat as a whale. He bought medicine for me, he helped me, he was even getting my teeth fixed. When I felt the urge to sniff glue again, I picked myself up and ran away from there and went back to the street.

One day he saw me in the street and came up to me and said, "What are you doing here, boy? Why don't you come back to my house with me?"

And I said, "I missed sniffing glue and I don't think I want to live in your house. Save that kindness for someone else."

Now, I think if I'd accepted his help I'd be a famous designer today, because he's known by society, by the important ladies of the city. But my head was thick, my heart was weak . . .

I was fifteen when I discovered the Casa de Passagem. It's a home for girls who live in the street. At the time, I was taking hormones, contraceptives, and they were very strong. My voice got higher, I even began to feel jealousy the way women feel it. I was very curious about the Casa de Passagem, I wanted to know how it worked, what the girls did there. I found out that the girls learned to crochet, to act, to dance, and to type. I stayed there for twenty-nine days. It was good there but I had a problem. Once a week six or seven different girls were taken to the gynecologist. When it was my turn, I said, "No, please!" I made a scene. I didn't want to go to the gynecologist. I told them I was afraid of doctors. I was eating so well in that place. There was cake, canjica, porridge . . . I didn't want them to find out I wasn't a girl.

But I had to tell them. "Lady, I'm not a girl," I said.

"What?"

"I'm a transvestite."

"Lift up your skirt."

So I lifted my skirt. That was when they understood what I meant. Even so, they forgave me. When I left they offered me a comb, scissors, a gown, and a blow dryer, so that I could cut hair.

But I didn't become a barber. I was out on the Avenida Conselheiro Aguiar and a car stopped. The driver called me over. I was wearing a red corset and a white shirt. He told me to open my shirt. He said, "That corset is very beautiful, I like the color, red is the color of sin, of desire. Do you have breasts?"

I was taking hormones at the time and I had little oranges.

"You look like a twelve-year-old girl," he said. "Get inside."

He asked me how much I charge. I said thirty.

"And what do you do?"

"Oral sex, anal sex. And if you want something fancy we can go to a five-star hotel. If you don't have much money, we can go somewhere cheaper."

"I want something special because it isn't just for me. If you wait five minutes I'll be right back."

So I stood there waiting for five minutes, and in exactly that amount of time he was back. He was very punctual. From the waist up, he looked like an executive, with a jacket and tie, but from the waist down he was naked. His wife was with him. She was dark-skinned and very beautiful.

"So let's get down to business, Aparecida. Are you active or passive?"

"Yes."

"Yes what?"

"I'm active and passive."

"You're both?"

"I'm both."

"That's good," he said. "Then let's go."

He took me to Eros. When we arrived at the front entrance to the motel, he told me to hide on the floor of the car, in the back, because only two clients were allowed to go into each room. They let us past the gate and the man parked in the garage, outside the room. It was a suite, with two levels, and upstairs there was no roof, so you could see the sky. I had never set foot anywhere like that. There was a menu and he asked me, "Are you thirsty?"

"Yes," I said.

He ordered dry martinis for himself and his wife and a Coke for me.

"Are you hungry?" he said.

"Yes."

He ordered something called lasagna. I had never eaten that kind of food before.

The woman said, "My love, would you like me to put on some music?"

He said yes.

She started dancing to the music and undressing. After a few minutes I saw that entire woman, undressed in front of me. I had only seen naked women in magazines. She was beautiful but even so, my member was no harder than a blade of grass.

"Are you embarrassed to undress?" the man asked me.

"No," I said, and I took off my shoes, my tights, my skirt, and then my blouse. He undressed too and the three of us went over to the bed. He told me to caress her breasts. I did what he told me to do. Then he said I should pour the rest of my Coca-Cola on her body. He began to lap up the drink. All I wanted was to get my money and leave.

He began to caress me and my member was still no harder than a blade of grass.

"Aparecida! Didn't you tell me you were active and passive."

"You asked me if I was active and passive, but you didn't tell me what those things meant. Tell me now, what is active and what is passive?"

"Active is the one who penetrates, passive is the one who receives."

"In that case, sir, I am the second thing. I only receive from behind. I don't get erections."

He sat there looking at me. Then he said, "Aparecida, would you like to open that box."

There was a box sitting on the table and I had been wondering what was inside. I thought it might be a present for me, some intimate apparel.

"Yes, I want to," I told him. I walked over and opened the box.

"Do you know what that is?" he said.

"It is a maranhão," I told him.

"People who haven't gone to school sometimes call it that, but the real name is a vibrador. Do you know how to use it?"

"I have seen in the magazines how sometimes people hold it in their hands, and sometimes they tie it to their waists."

"This is the kind you tie to your waist," he told me.

I did what he told me to do. The vibrator came attached to a pair of shorts. The man was paying. I have the habit of doing that, doing what the people who are paying tell me to do. I am afraid of them becoming angry, of not paying me, of taking me in their car to a dark forest, of leaving me there, dead, alive, alone . . .

*Sometimes they want to clean up the street during the day. There are little children, adults, old people, all in the street, and when people want to come into the center of the city and do their shopping, they aren't prepared for the sight of children sniffing glue, finishing themselves off on drugs, so they want to put us somewhere. For a while, a long time ago, they had a house we could go to during the day, where we could draw, have our hair cut, glue together popsicle sticks. That's what they thought we needed most of all, to make things with popsicle sticks. They might have run out of everything for us to do. There may have been no paper, no pens, toys, but they would have popsicle sticks. Somewhere there was a big factory making popsicle sticks that would never be stuck inside sugary frozen juice, that would never be licked. I didn't think this was right, so I once made an enormous tongue. No one knew what it was, there are a lot of people with no imagination, but there it was: popsicle sticks taking on the form of their destiny, to be inside the mouth of a child. At that place, they would feed us too, but at the end of the day, we would be sent back out into the street. The street had been clean during the day, and that is what they wanted. At night everyone who had a home went home.*

*I decided I didn't want to help them any more. I decided I would never go to that place again, that I would be in the street all day. I wanted to be where I wasn't wanted. Like plastic cups and straws, coconut shells, old paper bags, and chewed, discarded bubble gum, I was a form of waste. If that is what life had made me, I didn't want to be swept under the carpet.*

*The government started something they call the Lar Aberto, the Open Hearth, which is located on Floriano Peixoto. It is a place where they throw old ladies and children in together, old people who are too tired to get up and go to the bathroom so they do what they need to do right there, where they are. I went there once. It was raining and at that particular* moment, I had grown tired of being waste in the street. I threw in the towel and said, for tonight, they can sweep me into a corner.

That night an old woman was too weak to get up. Her mattress was soiled, she was soiled. "Lady," I said to the attendant, "help her."

She turned up her nose. "I have children at home. I change their diapers day and night. Do you think I want to clean the behind of an old lady who ought to know better?" She just sat there at her desk, reading a comic book.

So I lifted the lady in my arms and carried her to the shower. When you are a man inside a woman, you can do that.

I cleaned her and she thanked me. She was a tired woman.

When I discovered Cyana Cavalcante, I hadn't pleased a hundred men. I was new to the street. From time to time I would be taken by the police and put in FEBEM.

In FEBEM, when it was the time of day when it was morning, we would be led from the rooms where we slept to the showers. We would line up like little soldiers, go to the bathroom, take our showers and brush our teeth. Then we would have breakfast. Afterwards we had a recess that lasted an hour and a half. Finally, we would begin our different activities: drawing, painting, carpentry, hair cutting. Two or three different times I saw Cyana Cavalcante going to visit children. Every time she would come, I would call out to her, "Hey, lady, how are you?"

And she would say, "Fine, and you?"

One day she said, "What's your name?"

"Aparecida."

"Aparecida? Why is your name Aparecida?" She thought it was strange that my name was Aparecida. At FEBEM they had cut off all my hair, and on the outside there was little to suggest that part of me was a girl.

One day I climbed over the wall and I was no longer in FEBEM. I saw a sign in the city. I like to read signs. That one said, "Call this number to report an act of violence against a child." Because the only thing I saw all around me was violence, I decided to call.

"Hello," I said, "there is violence everywhere. And I'm a child."

"Child," said the person who answered the phone, "I think I recognize your voice. What is your name?"

"My name is Aparecida."

"I thought it was you."

I didn't know who she was, but soon she said, "I'm Cyana Cavalcante." I had been sniffing a lot of glue, but I remembered who she was.

"Oi tia . . . Hey ma'am," I said, "now I remember you."

*She invited me to visit her office.*

*When I would go, I would walk on top of the desks, throw papers around, insult the guards downstairs.*

*"Ô, Aparecida," she would say, "when I met you at FEBEM you were so well behaved. Why are you different now?"*

*"Because I am out of glue and out of food."*

*She was patient with me. So patient I started to like her. And when she said, "I don't think I deserve to be treated this way," I stopped to think about it. I decided she was right. There were only three parties who deserved to be treated that way: my stepfather, the police, and society.*

*So I began to behave around her. She would give me a piece of paper and a pencil and I would sit there drawing. She liked my drawings and she would always save them.*

*One day, I don't remember what year it was or how old I was, I was in the street by the Casa da Cultura and a reporter saw me there. She came up to me and asked me to tell her about my life. I started to tell her and she did something to my mind that made me want to tell her more and to perform for her. I posed seductively, walked in my underwear, unbuttoned my blouse, strutted across the Princess Isabel Bridge, and dove into the river wearing only a bra and panties. I did lots of things for her. She liked me and told me to tell her more about my life. I mentioned Cyana Cavalcante and she wanted to meet her. So I took the woman to meet her.*

*The two women, Cyana Cavalcante and the reporter, talked. When the reporter saw my drawings, she said that I ought to be given some sort of an opportunity in life, that I should be helped. She said that I should be allowed to exhibit my drawings.*

*Cyana Cavalcante liked the idea. She seemed to be thinking. She decided to organize a special event, a cocktail party and art exhibit, and she invited politicians and socialites. The reporter who had seen me in the street was there too, along with other reporters.*

*As people arrived they would say hello and shake my hand. As I shook their hands, I realized that I was shaking the hands of people I had seen on television: Jarbas Vasconcelos, Miguel Arraes, Dona Madalena, Geralda Farias, Olga Câmara . . . It gave me a strange feeling, as if I was there but not really there, as if the characters from a television program had escaped the inside of the TV and were posing as real people.*

I had a booth where they had displayed some of my drawings. I was not the only person whose works were being exhibited. There was also a sculptor and a poet, and each of them had their booths. They had put a paperweight on the table in each booth so that if someone wanted one of our works, they could place the money under the paperweight. The sculptor and poet were adults and they didn't live in the street. In fact they had never lived in the street. People would visit the booths of the sculptor and the poet but they wouldn't linger there. Everyone wanted to stand around my booth, have their picture taken and shake my hand. All of a sudden, I realized that it was not my drawings that were on display. I was on display. I was an animal, a monkey, an extraterrestrial.

"Excuse me, I have to go to the ladies' room," I said. I stood there in the ladies' room, lit up a cigarette and looked downstairs out the window. Outside there were some street children, all of them hungry and asking people as they walked in if they could spare some change. The people would all say, "Later, on my way out." Only they were really hoping that by that time the children would have gone somewhere else.

I went back to my booth and some people started to buy my drawings. The first people to buy pictures put the money under the paperweight. When there were a few bills there I took them and said, "Excuse me, I'm going to get some air."

The children were still outside, four of them. I gave them some money and bought myself some food. People had asked me why I lived in the street but no one asked if I was hungry. So I would talk with strangers about what it was like to be raped by your stepfather, about bleeding into your shorts, about the difficulty of walking under circumstances like that. But they would never ask me what I had eaten for lunch, whether I had eaten anything that day. Once I had bought myself some food and eaten it, I went to buy some pills in Coelhos. I stayed there for a few hours, sniffing glue and feeling the effects of the pills.

When I returned to the party, there were still some celebrities there, beautiful ladies with their hair pulled back in buns, ladies with jewelry and perfect noses, men in linen, men with ties.

I walked through the crowd and shouted, "The monkey is back." I climbed up on a table and scratched my armpit. I howled like Tarzan, jumped up and down.

*Today, when people walk by and see us and see only animals, I know they
have forgotten that they were once children, that some day they might
find themselves in a similar situation. Hungry children, mothers, grand-
mothers . . . There are artists lost in the street, beggars who speak eight
languages. But our suffering has weight. If every bit of anguish deserved
a tear, all of the tears together couldn't be contained by the banks of the
Capibaribe.*

There was another transvestite named Aparecida, only I didn't know that transvestite. The other Aparecida worked around the Praça do Diário, and one night her body was found in the dump near Coelhos. I don't know who killed her or why, only that her body was there, being eaten by ants and other insects, and that someone who was collecting bottles and cardboard in the dump found the body. On the radio they described the discovery of this transvestite, who happened to look like me. People in my neighborhood heard about it and thought I was dead. Everyone thought I was dead. If there's one thing I've discovered in life, it's that death doesn't change things very much. Sometimes, as a child, I had wondered whether the world would still exist if I died. This was sort of like a rehearsal, because as far as anyone knew, the Aparecida who woke up with her mouth full of ants was me.

I didn't know anything about this. I didn't know the other Aparecida was dead, I didn't know that she had ever been alive, and I didn't know that anyone thought I had gone to the other world. But one day I went to Bola na Rede and the first person to see me, a woman who sold vegetables, almost fainted.

"Aparecida," she said, "is that you?"

"Yes, Dona Elena, it's me." I thought she might have had trouble recognizing me because usually I would go home wearing pants, but that time I was wearing a skirt.

"Aparecida, the son of Dona Maria?"

"Aparecida, who is the son of Dona Maria but who would like to be the daughter of Dona Maria," I answered.

She came close and pinched me.

"Ouch," I said. "Why did you do that to me?"

"I thought you were dead."

"I'm alive, but if you want to kill me, pinching me like that is a good way to start."

"But your body was found in a dump. Your body was full of knife wounds."

I looked at my body. I had the same scars I always had.

"I would never lay my body down in a garbage dump. I only choose the best sidewalks to sleep on."

This time she laughed. She took me around the neighborhood so that everyone could see that I was alive.

I was happy to be alive, but I felt bad for the other Aparecida. Someone who looked like me, who had my name, who worked the way I worked, by selling her body, had been killed.

When Dona Elena took me to my house and knocked on the door, my mother was asleep in front of the television.

"Maria!" she said, "Maria, your son is alive."

"Of course he is," my mother said.

# THREE

**EATING IS A PROBLEM** for the man. Naked, sunburned, tied to a stake, he has an excruciating toothache. But that is the least of his worries: for weeks his Tupi-numbá captors have been arguing over just when this German harquebusier will be served up and who will have the honor of devouring which part of him. Hans Staden is getting thinner and Nhaepepo-oaçu will have none of it. The chief wants to know why the man with the red beard and ruddy cheeks seems to have no appetite. The prisoner speaks the chief's language but he merely points a finger at the inside of his mouth. The

Indian disappears for a time and returns brandishing a tool with which he plans to try his hand at dentistry. The unlucky traveler may have claimed that the pain has suddenly subsided but the chief is already splitting the man's gums, wrenching at the offending tooth. Nhaepepo-oaçu never manages to remove the tooth, but when he has given up he informs Hans Staden that it is time for him to eat or be eaten.

*Comer ou ser comido?* That is the puzzle with transvestites, Zoë thinks to herself as she puts aside the book about the unfortunate Teutonic adventurer and returns her thoughts to her writing. Eating is copulation in this country but copulation from a certain perspective: one copulates, or eats, by thrusting a penis into a hole. Only men can eat, and being eaten is the province of women. Not merely a means of procreation and of recreation, eating is creation plain and simple: being eaten is what makes one a woman. A girl becomes a woman as a result of being eaten just once. *She became a woman at thirteen*, you might hear, and everyone knows that that was the age when she lost her virginity. But it is not only the girl who can become a woman.

"*Ele me faz mulher na cama* . . . In bed, he makes me a woman," says Cleópatra Honey. Four transvestites—Cleópatra Honey, Lisete de Paris, Robertinha, and Aparecida—are sitting by the base of the flagpole on the Rua da Aurora. It is past midnight, the avenue is quiet, the rent-a-guard at the government building across the street is twirling his stick. This is the age of privatization.

"What do you mean?" Zoë asks.

"My boyfriend doesn't want to know anything about my member."

"He doesn't touch your penis?"

"*Vixe Maria* . . . Virgin Mary!" The others laugh. "The day he touches my stick, he can disappear forever. I won't let a *bicha* anywhere near my bedroom."

"What's wrong with queers?"

"*Bichas* are all right. I have a lot of friends who are *bichas*. But if he's in my bed and he's not paying me, he's a man. I like to feel like a woman."

"What makes you feel like a woman?"

They all look at Zoë with waning patience.

"When a man is a man." Cleópatra Honey says, in a playfully lusty voice. "When he desires me as a woman. It is something you can feel. He can desire you as a man and he can desire you as a woman. I like a man who likes to eat. If he's hungry for me and he eats me, I feel like a woman."

"What happens if one day he comes along and he wants to be eaten?" Zoë says.

"It means that all this time, he was only pretending to be a man, but inside he wants to be a woman. My boyfriend isn't like that. He knows how to make me a woman in bed."

"Are you a woman only in bed?"

"In bed, I'm a woman."

"And when you're not in bed?"

"I'm a transvestite."

"So you're a man?"

"On my birth certificate it may say that I am a man and that is the way God made me, but I know more about being a woman than Marilyn Monroe ever did."

"I have a lot of clients who are like that," Lisete de Paris interrupts. She is several steps behind in the conversation. "We all do. For every five who want to eat us, there are five who want to be eaten."

"And you eat them?"

"We're being paid."

"Do you like to eat them?"

"I do," says Cleópatra.

"You enjoy it?"

"I like to make them into women. I have my member, I use it, I enjoy. Those men hiding behind a mustache and a wife, I make them into women."

"But the others, the ones who make you a woman in bed, what are they looking for?"

"A woman."

"So why don't they go to a woman . . . to someone God made as a woman? There are plenty of women on the street."

"We have something they don't have," says Cleópatra Honey. "Brazilian women, they have a natural beauty, some of them at least, but they are not careful with their bodies. They don't wake up in the morning and immediately put on make-up; sometimes they don't wear make-up at all. They wear skirts, but are they certain the skirt they are wearing is the right one for them? Most of them will put on any piece of clothing you give them. We're more careful. We're made-up all the time."

"*Somos bonecas plastificadas* . . . We are plastic dolls," Lisete laughs, squeezing her swayless breasts.

"If you found a box full of money, would you do what Roberta Close did, have a sex change operation?" Zoë asks.

"Cut off my member?" she shrieks. The others laugh.

"Cut off your member in exchange for a vagina?"

"I can be eaten just fine as it is. Besides, this is the way God made me. I've taken things far enough already, living against the will of God."

"God doesn't like transvestites?"

"God made us in a certain way. Men are supposed to eat women."

In chapter 43 of *The True Story of the Ferocious Naked Man-Eating Savages found in the New World,* presented to Phillip I of Hessen in 1557, Hans Staden writes of a native chief who "had before him a great basket full of human flesh. At that moment he was eating the meat off a bone, which he held before my nose, asking if I would like a piece. I replied, 'Rarely will even an irrational animal devour those of its own kind. Why then would a man devour other men?' He took a bite and said, '*Jau ware sche*—I am a tiger, this is delicious.'"

Hans Staden may have had a tin ear for the language of the Tupinimbá and known little about the animals of Brazil—his "tiger," an animal not native to the country, was presumably a jaguar—but he had captured what four and a half centuries later would find a curious echo on the avenue where the rent-a-guard twirls his club, the odd car splutters by, a transvestite giggles. Like cannot eat like.

"Lesbians," Lisete tells Zoë, "all they do is make froth."

"What do you mean?"

"They just rub and make a lot of froth. No one eats anyone."

As Zoë returns to her apartment that night, she thinks only of eating Fátima.

## FÁTIMA LIVES IN A CAGE.

Thirty-three and childless, married for seven years, something is catastrophically wrong. Her husband can't get it up. But that isn't the official story.

On Sundays the clan gathers. The clan consists of her husband, her husband's two brothers and their children, her own sister, three nieces, and a maiden aunt. Sometimes they gather in Fátima's apartment, sometimes at her sister Selma's.

The men talk about soccer and whisky and rake the crooked politicians over the coals. They are against corruption. The women discuss dressmaking, interior decorating, music, food, soap operas, and corruption. They likewise oppose corruption. Every Brazilian is against corruption.

Walter drops his fork and Selma, Fátima's sister, gets up to look for a clean one.

"Zoë, we are the last of a generation," Fátima confides one day.

"What do you mean?"

"The sort of women who live like this."

"Like what?"

"Who have to go to the kitchen for a clean fork because our husband dropped his."

"Why don't you send him?"

An expression somewhere between disbelief and resentment.

"Could you talk about these things?"

"If we talk, it's worse."

"So what do you do?"

"Look for a clean fork."

"I mean, what do you do about the things you want but cannot get?"

"I look at the sea."

Zoë looks at the sea too but it returns the image of Fátima. The waves breaking against the shore at high tide remind her of a rhythm perfected beneath the sheets. When the tide of depression recedes, something must take its place. In Zoë's case it is libido. Melancholy is about falling, living is about grabbing on. Desire is giving her a toehold in life.

Fátima arrives at Zoë's apartment one morning bearing a large piece of cake. Fátima bakes cakes. It is something she does in the afternoons, when her husband is home from work. He works only in the morning. The mornings are hers.

Married women can visit single women in their homes, unsupervised. It is a fact that makes Zoë think life is worth living. Fátima visits once or twice a week.

She speaks in a way you cannot speak in English, a language that depends on the establishment of explicit perspectives. In English, you must ask what your partner in conversation does and where he or she is from. Fátima has never quite asked Zoë why she came here, how long she will be here this time, why she has come back. She is simply talking and Zoë is talking (though mostly she is listening and watching how the woman holds her cigarette, how she punctuates her speech with the most subtle movements of the lines in her face, the cross of her legs, the angle at which her instep becomes her foot).

Fátima's hands were the first part of her that Zoë desired. Five slender fingers, perfectly articulated, fragile. Zoë wanted to protect those fingers, to be protected by them. The nails, it seems to Zoë, meet the cuticles in a way that suggests a delicate disharmony, like something we want and do not want to happen.

"*É de maracujá.*" She offers Zoë a big wedge of passion fruit cake, about a quarter of the entire production. The name in Portuguese is more appropriate. There is nothing passionate about this fruit.

It has a mildly sedative effect. On the other hand, a cake made by Fátima is in itself an erotic event. Zoë takes a small bite as she looks at Fátima's shoulders.

Doutor Inácio had informed Zoë that most people who use selective serotonin reuptake inhibitors experience a marked decrease in sexual interest. The loss of interest, he reassured her, would last only as long as the course of treatment. "The effects on the libido are completely reversible." On the other hand, a small portion of patients experience just the opposite, a heightened interest in sex, the desire to flirt with strangers or make sexual advances in contexts that would normally be inappropriate. He told her to watch for this; it could be a sign that the drug was ushering in a state of unnatural elation. Although there is no proof of this, he had said, it is even possible that the drug can induce mania.

Zoë is patently elated but has no intention of declaring this to be a problem to doutor Inácio or anyone else. Desire, she has discovered on an Internet health site, has something to do with dopamine, a neurotransmitter. She doesn't quite know what a neurotransmitter is. Synapses: THE LOCUS AT WHICH THE NERVOUS IMPULSE PASSES FROM THE AXON OF ONE NEURON TO THE DENDRITES OF ANOTHER HAVING THE FORM OF AN ACTUAL BOUNDARY BETWEEN THE TWO NERVE FIBERS OR POSSIBLY ONLY A SURFACE OF CONTACT AND CONSTITUTING THE POLARIZING AND SELECTIVE ELEMENT TYPICAL OF MOST OF THE NERVOUS SYSTEMS OF THE HIGHER ANIMALS, the dictionary on her computer informs her. Her neurotransmitters, synapses—whatever they are—seem to be working perfectly, better than ever. If this is the result of a tiny blue pill, what better invention has science brought us? Ever? And since when is the almost irrepressible desire to make love a chemical reaction in the brain gone wrong?

The official story is that Fátima is undergoing treatment for infertility.

"Your husband has you say that?"

"Yes."

Nothing makes Zoë happier than the fact that Fátima's husband is impotent, but she says, as if hopefully, "Are the prospects good that the doctors can do something for him?"

"He tried some pills, but they gave him palpitations."

"Oh," Zoë says, just above the pounding in her own chest.

"Those pills gave him his first erection in years, but we couldn't enjoy it. He thought he was going to have a heart attack."

"This cake is delicious."

"He wants to try spiritual surgery."

"Spiritual surgery?"

"Yes."

"What's that?"

"That's when a spirit performs the operation."

"Who performs the operation?"

"A famous physician, doutor Fritz. The problem is finding the right medium."

"The right medium?"

"Doutor Fritz, the German doctor, you've never heard of him? He died a long time ago, and now several mediums claim to have access to his skills."

"What does this dead doctor know about erections?"

"Are you laughing at me?"

"No," Zoë says, honestly. The rules are different in this country. There are contexts where the most Cartesian of observers will embrace a different logic. Pierre Verger, the French ethnologist and photographer, spent most of his life in Bahia living among practitioners of spirit possession. When asked by fellow anthropologist John Ryle if he believed in spirits, he answered with an unmistakable air of sadness, "I'm too French for that. Reason puts paid to everything, to every opportunity for pleasure, relaxation, the truest expressions of sentiment." But, he added, "I live as if I believed."

Whatever the extent of doutor Fritz's expertise with erectile dysfunction, it would be just fine with Zoë if Fátima's husband never found the right medium.

"Why don't you have some cake with me?" she asks. Although she'd like to eat the whole piece herself, sharing some will allow her to see Fátima's mouth move, her jaws open, close. The purse of her lips.

"I'm on a diet."

"You?" Zoë says, astonished.

"I'm overweight."

"How can you say that?"

"Look at me." Funny, Zoë thinks, she has suggested the one thing I haven't stopped doing from the moment she walked through the door.

"There would be less of you if you lost any weight. Please, have some cake."

Fátima laughs and accepts a small piece.

Watching her eat is even better than Zoë had anticipated. For one thing, the movement of her lips as she chews is slow, gentle; this cake, at once sweet from the sugar, tart from the fruit, makes her cheeks pucker. She picks up the last crumbs and licks her fingers.

Zoë wants to be one of those fingers.

"My husband is going away to Fortaleza next week, on business."

Zoë feels more than elated. She believes in spirits. "I'm sure you're going to miss him. You'll have to visit me more often. We could go out, to the movies . . ."

"Do you know how long it has been since I saw a movie?"

"No."

"Neither do I."

Fátima's husband, and hence Fátima, doesn't leave the house after sunset. No one has explained why they are always home after dusk, but there is no reason to ask. There may be no place on earth where fear of the dark is not an infantile regression but a generalized state of mind. Lack of public lighting is a leading topic of protest in letters to the editor of the local newspapers and nothing inspires more fear than a dark alley or, worse still, a quiet forest. Even the reflection of the moon, dissevering and fusing over the ocean, has been forbidden: all along the waterfront, floodlights are switched on at dusk. Anyone in Northeast Brazil with anything to lose is hiding behind high walls topped with razor wire, the tinted windows of automobiles, a life of avoidance.

"What do you do in the evening?"

"In the evening?"

"When you are at home in the evening."

"We have supper."

"So you eat?"

"We eat. Then my husband watches television. Sometimes I watch with him. Other times I sit on the terrace. I like to read."

"Would you like some more cake?"

When Fátima leaves, Zoë imagines the cake crumbled across her body, tiny pieces like grains of sand scattered across the small of her back, around her shoulder blades, inside the gentle curves at the backside of her knees. Zoë thinks what it would be like to gently move Fátima's hair to the side, exposing the back of her neck . . . With her lips, Zoë gently explores one vertebra after another, collecting the scattered crumbs and a sense of the taste of Fátima's skin. She had wanted to be the cake that Fátima was eating, now she was eating from Fátima's body.

Fátima is sitting up now. She has a high hairline, very high, but where the hair begins it is voluminous, black. Zoë feels Fátima's hair between her fingers. Fátima is looking somewhere else.

If an extraterrestrial were to arrive on our planet and examine our bodies, the ear would probably be considered the ugliest human appendage. Ears are a malformation we happen to have grown accustomed to through a force of habit that makes us indifferent to the abomination. So why this impulse to kiss Fátima's ears? Unlike any other set of ears she has ever seen, there is a certain grace to Fátima's. Zoë runs the hair on the left side of Fátima's head behind her ear and brings her lips to the lobe. But the woman moves away. She turns, turns toward Zoë. Now she is running her hands through Zoë's hair, looking at her. Or is it through her? Her fingertips brushing against Zoë's scalp.

Her lips are coming toward Zoë's. This she hadn't anticipated. But the lips do not arrive and what she hadn't expected doesn't happen. Fátima's mouth touches down not on Zoë's mouth but on her frozen eyelids. Fátima's hands, no longer on her own shoulders but on Zoë's, are toying with her blouse. When Fátima's lips finally arrive at Zoë's mouth she is unfastening the buttons, then kissing her way down Zoë's chest, slowly. Slowness. That is what men do not understand. They are so eager to arrive the journey means nothing to them. If it weren't for that shortcoming, Zoë, thinks, I wouldn't mind having a man now and then.

When Fátima reaches Zoë's navel, she presses her lips around it, explores with her tongue the part of her that once led to her mother.

Hans Staden, Nhaepepo-oaçu, Cleópatra Honey, what do they know about the possibilities of like eating like?

ANOTHER NIGHT by the flagpole on the Rua da Aurora. It is late, very late. No one except Rogéria has had any luck on the avenue. Aparecida is holding the tape recorder and asking the questions.

*Arlene, do you practice prostitution por sobrevivênvia ou por esporte . . . as a means of survival or for fun?*

I practice prostitution as a hobby.

*As a hobby?*

Yes, because in my house, there is enough to eat. My parents know that I am gay, but they don't know that I am a transvestite. The money I make is for myself.

*So you do it for the money, to have money for yourself?*

I do it for the money, but I also do it because I like it. It's nice when you like your work.

*You like your work?*

I like to meet men.

*Are all of your clients men?*

Some of them aren't. Some of them are queer. Those are the ones I make into women.

Perhaps the most curious thing about the transvestites of this city is that they revile homosexuals. Male clients who want to be penetrated are the stuff of endless ridicule. Not "real" men but closet homosexuals, these are the clients who want the experience transvestites say they seek, to be women in sex. Transvestites respect only "real" men.

"*Môna, peguei um macho com um pau tão grande* . . . Honey, I got myself a man with the biggest stick!" Roberta de Roma announces proudly. Delighted (or is it envious?), Erica wants to know just how big. They proceed to compare the endowments of their respective conquests. This most regressive, most heterosexual of fantasies goes unchallenged: the bigger the better. If it causes pain, so be it. Suffering is intrinsic to womanhood.

But are these the myths that explain Aparecida? Or is there something different about her? That she sleeps in the street and the other transvestites in homes or boardinghouses does not account for the extent of her peculiarity. The other transvestites use their members, as they put it, and they find pleasure in their work. Or so they say. Aparecida cannot make her clients into women. She is as impotent as Fátima's husband.

"The others say they like having sex with clients," Zoë mentions to her one day. "Do you?"

"When they are penetrating me, I try to think about something else. About the river, about the trees. Sometimes it makes me sick to my stomach. But at the same time, I am working, so I must concentrate. The clients are asking for a fantasy, and it is what I give them. Otherwise they go away dissatisfied. So at the same time, I must talk with them."

The women prostitutes, do they like the sex?

"They do it to support their children."

Would they do it if they didn't have children to support?

"Only if they needed the money."

"So maybe you are more like the women prostitutes."

"I think I am more like a leaf on the river."

**"DO YOU LIKE THIS DRAWING?"** Zoë had recently given Aparecida some stencils.

A striking, confident woman, behind her a tiny police car, a park bench, a pocket-sized client. The self is very large, but the economy, the landscape, the representatives of authority are inevitable fixtures.

"A lot."

She shows Zoë another one. As if to illustrate Philippe Ariès's arguments about the iconography of children in medieval European art, the child sucking a pacifier at the doors of the department store is a miniature adult. Ariès argued that until the eighteenth century, Europeans had little notion of children as anything but small adults. There was nothing distinctive about their style of dress, their games, and from the age they were physically capable of work, they would be at their parents' side in the fields. Aparecida's infants wear lipstick and tight skirts.

But there is more. Zoë discovers that on the back of the drawing Aparecida has been writing. The writing begins there, behind the drawing, but it continues onto other sheets. It is almost impossible for Zoë to make out the script, so she has Aparecida read it into the tape recorder.

### Friday, 10 August

I wake up at four in the morning, and like every day I go to the Rua da Aurora to wait for Dona Rebeca, a lady with a good heart who always helps me. I wait for Dona Rebeca to come down from her apartment. Whenever she can, she brings food for my dog and for the three dogs of a lady who has been living in the street for a long time. At five thirty Dona Rebeca comes down from the apartment where she lives to walk her dog. She carries two bags, one with the dog food and another one for me, which contains things for my personal hygiene—two bars of soap, some rose-petal cream, perfume. I walk around with her and her dog until six in the morning. As I am walking with her, she gives advice . . .

At eight o'clock in the morning I go to the Rua do Lima, to Dona Maria's house for breakfast. After breakfast, I and the other homeless people who have also come to eat stop and listen to the word of God, which Dona Maria explains to us. When she finishes telling us what is inside the Bible, she tells us to take the clothing she has for us. Next she gives us some pamphlets with the word of God, for us to read and think about. Then each of us goes our own way.

I go to the Rua da Aurora to take a bath and wash my clothing, and when I finish I walk around a little to see if I can come up with some money. I go to the Praça Maciel Pinheiro because there are some people there who give me things. At the Matriz da Boa Vista Church, there's a girl who helps me. Her name is Zilda. She is the secretary in the church and she is very generous. She gives me some change, which is enough for a snack.

At night, I see Dona Vera of the Livraria Brandão. Dona Vera gives me a bag of food so I'll have something to eat. I thank her and go back to the Rua da Aurora. When I arrive in the Rua da Aurora, I sit down and start crocheting for a while, to pass the time. I distract myself to avoid the temptation to get high.

When it gets dark, I continue to walk around for a while, waiting to get sleepy. And when I am sleepy, I go over to the backside of the Legislative Assembly to sleep. I pick up some papers and put them on the sidewalk in front of the pharmacy that's across the street from the Legislative Assembly.


**Saturday, 11 August**
This morning I woke up and the dogcatchers were taking away my dog and the other street dogs. I went to ask them to let my dog go.

They wouldn't listen. I insisted. They didn't like my insistence and threatened to have me arrested.

When Aparecida is done reading into the tape recorder, Zoë walks across the Rua da Aurora to the stationery store and buys a notebook. How could I have forgotten? she laments. Aparecida knows how to read and write. Zoë gives her the notebook and asks her to write in it that night. To continue writing, just as she has begun, recording her reflections on what she sees in the street. In the meantime, Aparecida continues to talk with the machine.

*He was a soldier at the Treze de Maio Battalion. He came to me one night, to pay for my services. I did what he paid me to do. He came to look for me again the next night, and then on other nights. His name was Marcílio. I went to live in his house. I ironed, washed, cooked. I was learning what the daily life of a woman is like, to wake up early in the morning . . .*

*When he took me to his house, he introduced me to his mother. "Mother, this is my girlfriend."*

*I didn't like that, because he seemed to be deceiving her. One day the old woman came up to me and said, "It is good that you are with my son. He has been with a lot of women, but he has never been happy with any of them. And none of them gave him a child. Will you give him one?"*

*My chest tightened its grip around my heart. I turned to her and said, "Dona Severina, I cannot give your son a child. I am not a woman."*

*"You are not a woman?"*

*"No, I am not a woman."*

*"You are not a woman today and you were not a woman the day you walked into my house, but you are the only honest person my son has ever been with."*

*"If you knew I was not a woman, why did you ask me for a grandchild?"*

*"I wanted to know if you were the person I thought you were."*

*"Aparecida," he asked me, "Are you jealous of women?"*

*"No," I said. "Women are what inspire me to be what I am." But then*

I added, "So if you ever betray me, Marcílio, betray me with a woman. If you deceive me with a transvestite, I cannot say what I will do."

Time passed. One day his mother came to me and gave me some money. "Throw a party for my son. We haven't had a party for a long time."

I cooked feijoada and dobradinha and other dishes. He invited some friends of his from the barracks and some women. When it was a certain hour of the night, everyone left for their houses, everyone except one woman. She stayed.

I told her, "It is very late, you can stay here, in the living room."

I gave her a sheet and Marcílio and I went to the bedroom. But he was strange, distant. Later in the night he got up and went to the living room and began to stroke her legs. I could see him from the bedroom. So I went out to speak with him.

"Marcílio," I said. "Do you desire her?"

"Yes," he answered.

So I put lipstick on her lips, perfume on her shoulders, and I lent her some underwear that Marcílio liked. I gave them my bed, and in the morning I made eggs and coffee and brought the food to them.

Marcílio asked if the expression on my face meant that I was angry or jealous.

"No," I said. "I am not angry and I am not jealous. You kept your promise."

"How can you let him cheat on you?" people in the neighborhood would ask. They ridiculed me.

But I didn't see it the way they did. "I am a woman in bed, but not before God. I cannot give him a child, and if I am going to lose him, I want to lose him to a woman."

But I didn't lose him to that woman. He stayed with me. For staying with me, I called him every dirty word I could think of. The girl was a virgin and I thought it was his obligation to stay with her.

Women from the neighborhood would come to me and I would pluck their eyebrows, do their nails. Marcílio asked me, "Do you know how to cut hair?"

"Yes," I said.

"So cut mine."

"I am tired, Marcílio. I have been looking after the house all day. I'll cut your hair on Saturday. In any case, in a while I need to braid the hair of sixteen girls. Your aunt is having a party, all the girls want their hair done. Don't you remember?"

He became angry and went to see Piná, a chubby transvestite who had visited me a few times. People would go to Piná to have their hair cut. For payment, Piná would often prefer sex over money.

I went to braid the hair of the sixteen girls, something that takes a long time. When I returned to the house, it was locked from the inside. I knocked on the door. "Marcílio," I said, "I'm tired, I want to take a shower. Open the door."

"There's no one at home," a voice said. It was Marcílio's.

"Oxente . . . Hey," I said, "if there's no one at home, why would you be there to tell me that?"

There was no reply.

"Who's in there with you?" I asked.

"No one. But you can break down the door if you want."

He didn't think I could break down the door. But if there's one thing I know it's that if a person wants to be calm, he is calm, if a person wants to be good, he is good, and if he wants to be violent, he is violent. I wanted to be violent.

I kicked the door, but it didn't open. I kicked it again, and still it didn't open. I went to a neighbor's house and picked up a hoe. With the hoe I broke down the door.

Piná was on all fours and Marcílio was penetrating him from behind.

"Marcílio," I said, "I told you you could betray me with a woman. Why did you have to choose this fat little faggot."

Piná wasn't saying anything but he started to laugh.

There was a duck squatting on a shelf, a duck made of clay. I picked up the duck and smashed it over Piná's head. His head didn't split in two as I had hoped, but Piná ran out of the bedroom and out of the house. He was wearing nothing but a sheet, screaming, bleeding.

Marcílio ran for the bedroom door, but I closed it before he had a chance to escape.

I'd been violent enough for one day, so I said, "Marcílio, let's have a conversation."

"I don't have anything to talk about with you."

"You're going to have to find something to say."

But it was true. He had nothing to say to me. He slapped me. Whenever I'm slapped, I think of my stepfather, so I became violent again. I hit him, he hit me. There wasn't another clay duck around to smash over his head, so I ran to the kitchen and picked up a knife. I slashed his arm. It was something I shouldn't have done. He tried to grab the knife from me and even though he didn't take it away, an accident happened. Before I knew it my ribs were bleeding. We were both bleeding, and crying.

I cleaned his wound, then my own.

That night I didn't sleep in his bed. I pretended I was going to sleep on the couch. But as soon as I knew he was asleep, I collected my things and went back into the city.

### Wednesday, 17 August

Construction workers and the police were beating some people who live in the Rua da Aurora. Two policemen were hitting a pregnant woman.

I went up to a policeman and told him that the woman was pregnant, but even so he didn't stop hitting her. I told him I was going to report him on the radio, but still he continued to hit her. He got angry at me and when he finally stopped, it was to strike me. He hit me twice in the face and told me to disappear from that place. I was afraid and I went away. The passersby were revolted by what they were seeing, but they couldn't do anything.

When the men were finished with what they were doing, they went away, but they threatened to come back at night, to settle scores with me and with the other girls who stay around there. That night the girl lost the baby she was expecting.

### Thursday, 18 August

On Thursday I got up at eight o'clock in the morning and went to the Rua da Aurora to take a bath. When I finished, I went to the Rua do Lima, to Dona Maria's house for breakfast. And after breakfast, I went to the Praça Maciel Pinheiro to get some money so I could buy some cleaning products. My clothing was dirty. I went to the Matriz da Boa Vista Church. I got some money from the secretary and then I went to the Livraria Brandão to see the owner, because she likes me and helps me whenever she can. I spent a few hours talking with her and when it was noon she gave me some spare change so I could buy myself something to eat. I thanked her and continued on my way.

It was four o'clock in the afternoon when I arrived at the Rua das Ninfas. I sat down on the sidewalk in front of a store to crochet and pass the time. I crocheted until eight o'clock at night. When it was eight thirty, I got up and went to the Rua da Aurora to sleep because I was very tired and had a headache. I went to the place I normally sleep, behind the Legislative Assembly, and sat on the sidewalk under the awning. I took out my notebook to draw and I drew until three o'clock in the morning.

I couldn't fall asleep.

A police van passed by and the policemen were chasing two street girls. I got up and, hiding in a tree, observed them from a distance, to see what they wanted with the girls. Two policemen grabbed them and made them go down to the edge of the river. When the girls went down there, two more policemen came along. They ordered them to take off their clothing and started having sex with the girls. They ordered them to practice oral sex and while the girls were doing that one of the other policemen penetrated one of them from behind.

I was unlucky because the branch I was sitting on and witnessing that barbarity from broke. When the policemen realized that someone was watching what they were doing with the girls, they ran after me and grabbed me. They asked what I was doing there and, because I didn't have an alibi, I made one up. I told them I was waiting for my boyfriend. But it didn't do any good because they didn't believe me and they hit me and pushed me inside the van, saying they were going to take me to the police station. But they didn't take me there. They took me to the underside of a bridge. When we got there, they opened the door and told me to begin sucking. One of them was pointing a gun at my head. When I finished doing what they had asked me to do they hit me a few times and ordered me to take off my clothing. Then they told me to run away in my underwear. I did what they told me to do. In my underwear, I ran, wondering, what had they done to the girls . . .

I ran until I was very tired and I stopped in front of a house and picked up some pages of a newspaper from the trash and covered myself. I stayed there in front of the house until six in the morning.

When it was six o'clock, the lady of the house came to me and asked how long I had been there. I told her I had been there a long time. She asked me why I was dressed like that.

When I explained why I was dressed in the pages of the newspaper, the woman understood me. She was disturbed by the things I told her. Her son was a policeman. She had a sad expression on her face and then she asked if I was hungry. I told her I was. She went into her house for a cup of coffee and two pieces of bread and she also gave me a pair of shorts and a T-shirt. She asked me if I had bus fare to get back to the city and I told her I didn't. The lady gave me two reais. I thanked her.

I walked to the bus stop and waited along with the other people who were also going into the center of the city. All of a sudden, I noticed that one of the people waiting for the bus was a policeman, one of the ones who had taken me under the bridge. I invoked my *pombajira*, the messenger of a spirit, who obscured his vision. The man didn't recognize me.

When the bus arrived I passed right in front of the policeman and he didn't recognize me. I passed through the turnstile on the bus and took the first seat I found. Arriving in the city, I went back to the Rua da Aurora, to get some water to take a bath and then to go about my work.

*A man drove past. I was standing on the corner of Mário Melo and the Rua da Aurora. He drove past once, slowly, looked at me, and continued on his way. But then a few minutes later he was back. He pulled up to the curb and said, "Will you give me a lot of pleasure?"*

*"Yes," I told him, "so long as you give your fantasies the freedom they are entitled to."*

*He told me that in that case I should get into his car.*

*I sat in the front, next to him. A crucifix was hanging from the mirror, swaying as he drove. He said we should go somewhere special, to Senzala. I had never been to that motel but I told him I thought that was a good idea. We drove along Mário Melo and across Agamenon Magalhães. We reached Rosa e Silva and then took different streets I didn't know. When we got to a certain point, the police stopped him. They were stopping everyone.*

*The man opened the window. The policeman looked at the man and looked at me. He asked for the man's documents. He opened his wallet and handed the policeman his registration but that wasn't the only thing he gave. He also put a fifty real bill along with the papers.*

*The policeman took the documents away and came back in a few moments to return them.*

*"Is this your daughter?" the policeman asked, looking at me.*

*The man didn't say anything.*

*"Are you going to answer?"*

*"This is not my daughter," the man said.*

*"Is this your wife?"*

*Another policeman came over and said, "No, I think they're twin sisters."*

*The man was bald and a bit fat. I didn't like the comment.*

*The first policemen asked, "Can I see your documents?"*

Because I don't have any, I said, "I don't have any. I lost them in a fire."

"You look like you have been exposed to a lot of heat," the other policeman said. "So does your sister."

They asked the man to step out of the car. He was gone for a long time. When he came back he said that the police had made him write a check for a thousand reais. They weren't content with the fifty he had already given them. Otherwise, they had told him, his name would appear in the newspapers and they would call his wife.

The man started the car and drove away but in another direction. He was shaking. When we got to a certain place, he shouted, "Get out of the car!"

I didn't know where we were. I'd never been on that street before and I didn't want to get out. I said, "Take me back where you found me."

"I found you in hell," the man told me." I'm not going back there. Get out of my car."

So I got out of his car. It was raining. My shoes were sinking in the mud.

*How do I ask for food in a bar? I say, "Good afternoon. How are you?
I was wondering if you have any leftover food."*

*If you speak to people that way, they respect you and a lot of them
will give you food. They'll say, "Come back at two o'clock. Come back at
two-thirty." And when you come back, they have some food for you.*

*I get water over there on the Rua do Lima. I carry it in a bucket and I
find a hidden spot and take my bath. I used to bathe in the public bath on
Dantas Barreto, but not anymore. I'm not roaming over there now. Now
I'm here, on this side of the river. Over there it's difficult because sometimes there's no water. So I take my bath and when I'm finished, I wash
my clothing. Then I hide my things and I sit down for a while.*

*At the edge of the water, your only company is the little crabs. So if I've
taken my bath and it's six thirty or seven I walk along the street and stop
at houses to ask for breakfast. I try to go to different houses. I don't like to
always be bothering the same people. There are people with a good heart
and when they can, they give me a banana, a piece of bread, a roll, one
thing or another. I've eaten so I take my ball of yarn. Someone ordered
a skirt for twelve reais, which isn't much, but at least it's enough to buy
shampoo, cream, and toothpaste, some deodorant to rub around the
armpits. I'm making it for her, for a girl who lives over there, a fourteen-
year-old. I started yesterday and I haven't gotten very far. On Wednesday,
I'll give it to her. Then I'll be able to buy a few things and clean myself up
a little.*

*Last night I was in a friend's house, at Dona Inalda's, watching some
television. She lives over in Santo Amaro. We were watching a soap. Then
I came here and was crocheting near the Torture Never Again statue.
Later I went walking around in the street, to have a look at the monuments.*

*The street is a place where you are accompanied and alone. Everyone can be watching you and you are alone, and you can be alone and find, suddenly, that you are accompanied. Lucielo was a boy from the countryside. He came to the city, to Recife, and I looked after him because he was very little. And all of a sudden, he fell in love with me. All he wanted was to be at my side. But I didn't feel the same passion for him. I looked at him and I saw a child, I saw myself when I was younger. Sometimes I would be sleeping and then I would feel that tiny thing of his rubbing against me; I would turn and slap him. He would become angry, but I wouldn't give him what he wanted, I wouldn't do what others had done to me when I was his age.*

*There was Seu Gervásio too. He was not just a client I had sex with, there was more; he was someone I looked to as a father, because he gave me presents, clothing, paid for my stay in a pension near the wharves. We would talk a lot and I would ask him how things were with his wife. Many times he would come to me and tell me that he had fought with his wife. He would ask me what I would do if I were in his shoes, if I were a man and had a wife and children, what I would do to win back my wife. Because I knew that a lot of women are romantic and like to receive flowers and a box of chocolates, I told him what to buy. So I think he liked that and he came to think of me as a person he could talk with in his times of need. I didn't just give him pleasure because he was paying, I gave him a sort of comfort. That is what brought him close to me.*

*My family is a source of loneliness. I have a sister, Sônia, who lives in Aguazinha, and a brother, Marcos, who lives in São Paulo. I am the third child of my mother and my father. Marcos, when he can, he sends a letter to my mother and sometimes money. A little now and then. My sister helps too, helps my mother. But they are people I don't have access to.*

*My sister has children and she doesn't think it is good for me to be in her house, because her children might get ideas, try to imitate my feminine appearance. When we were at home together my brother would try to tell me not to flip my wrist the way I would, not to play with dolls. My sister was different, she would even give me her underwear. But when she left the house, she no longer wanted me to be the way I am.*

*In the street, we don't live, we just exist. There are too many sleepless nights, hungry nights, and then the police come. Sometimes we aren't doing anything, they make us get out from under the shop awnings. Sometimes they hit us because we're sleeping on the sidewalk outside a store, or else the owner throws a bucket of water on us.*

"Aparecida," Zoë says one day, "You have a tattoo that reads, 'Amor só de mãe'—There's no love like mother love—what does that mean for you?"

"It is a reminder that we shouldn't be deceived by other sorts of love we might find in life. Only in a mother will you find a lap to rest your head in, the possibility of being heard and understood. So today, if I had to fall in love . . . I think I could only fall in love with my mother's love. That is why I decided to write that on my body."

"But your mother . . ."

"Could you buy me a cigarette?"

### 3 September

I woke up with a fever and headache. It was eleven in the morning and I walked over to the Rua da Aurora where I separated my clothing into two piles, but before beginning to do the wash I went to Dona Maria's to see if she would give me something to eat. She was at home and she gave me a cup of coffee and two pieces of bread. Back at the Rua da Aurora, I washed my clothing. The headache was still with me, so I took the fifty cents I had and bought some aspirins. I lay down to see if the pills would have any effect. After a while, I was asleep and when I woke up it was nine in the evening. I walked around for a while and then it was eleven and I was still sleepy, even though I usually am most awake at night. So I went to the spot where I sleep, outside the Legislative Assembly, but discovered that someone had defecated there. I was very tired and wanted to go to sleep, so I got two empty bottles from the trash and asked the guard at Treze de Maio to fill them with water so I could wash down the sidewalk. I had to make a lot of trips back and forth and every time the guard made me wait. When I finished, it was one thirty in the morning. I stayed up for a while, to see if the evangelicals, who bring food every Thursday night, would show up. I had to wait a long time but at two thirty they came and distributed food and spoke to me and other people in the street about God. At three I prayed, to thank God for the people who had helped me that day and soon I was asleep.

*In the past, women weren't very concerned with beauty. You would arrive in someone's home, in a manor house, and see those beautiful ladies with their hair gathered in a bun, their lips the color that God made them, their cheeks as natural as if they had woken up at that very moment. Women didn't make great sacrifices, they didn't suffer for their beauty. After lipstick was introduced by Max Factor and eyeliner by Christian Dior, the idea that a woman could be a painted object came to be accepted; and women became more conscious of those things. So did we, because for us, women are a point of reference, an inspiration. If I know how to cross my legs, walk, hold a cigarette, it is because I have studied women.*

*On Sundays, near the Praça Joaquim Nabuco, the members of an evan-*
*gelical church used to come to talk with us, to tell us about the word*
*of God, and to bring us a snack: hotdogs with ketchup, mayonnaise,*
*and grated cheese. They would also give us clothing. And in exchange*
*for those things, they would ask us to visit the church. One day I went*
*and as I arrived they were exorcising the spirit from the body of an old*
*woman. The lady's* pombajira *was revealing itself, saying that it wanted*
*to take her life, that it had already pushed her body in front of a car*
*and dropped from a construction site a hammer that almost fell on her*
*head. The woman's* pombajira *went away and then it was my turn. The*
*pastor asked me my name. After saying my name was Aparecida, the*
*only thing I remember is that my legs hurt, my spine hurt, my eyes went*
*dark. Darkness was everywhere. When I woke up I was in another room,*
*people were running a cloth with rubbing alcohol across my forehead. A*
*woman was kneading my fingers. I asked what had happened. She told*
*me that a* pombajira *by the name of Cigana had fled my body. After it*
*left my body, the spirit explained that it had been following my footsteps*
*from the time I was nine, that it was waiting until I turned thirteen to*
*possess me. Because I never prepared myself by finding out which* pombajira *could protect me, Pombajira Cigana had come to possess me, to*
*bring out my feminine side. My feminine side has been with me from the*
*cradle, but it is the* pombajira *that makes it come out. So if the spirit*
*tells me to wear an earring and I put one on, it is as if I were putting*
*the earring on the spirit. If I comb my hair, it's as if I were combing the*
*hair of the spirit. But this* pombajira *wanted to take my life. It was this*
*spirit that made me fall off the back of a bus once. I was hanging onto*
*the back bumper and it loosened my grip, sent me crashing down on the*
*street.*

*I have two dogs. I call one of them Charlotte. The other one is Sharon Stone, because she likes to lift her leg. That trait of hers made me think of the film where Sharon Stone has a special way of crossing and uncrossing her legs.*

*Dona Rebeca helps a lot, giving food for the dogs, but there are a lot of street dogs around here. Fia, a lady who lives in the street, is raising eight dogs. So when Dona Rebeca gives me a bag of food, I set some aside for Sharon Stone and some for Charlotte, and I give the rest to Fia, for her dogs. But some days mine have nothing to eat, just a bone or whatever people in the bars will give.*

*The good thing about dogs is that you can be certain that if you feed yours, if you take care of him, he won't betray you, say bad things about you, bed your wife. Sometimes you put your money on certain people, you believe in them, but their minds become polluted and they want to take advantage of you. Even at the worst of times, a dog will stay at your side.*

That man sitting there, he isn't the type of man whose fantasy it is to take a woman to a motel and have sex with her. He isn't a sadist, he isn't a masochist. His pleasure is different. He likes to watch. He sits there, at the edge of the river, and when a prostitute takes a client into the swamp, he watches. That is what gives him pleasure. So this is how it is: everyone has their own way of looking, of watching. Some people cover themselves with mud and hide among the mangrove trees, others climb trees, still others aren't content to watch from a distance and they want to get closer. This is the Motel Manguezal, the Mangrove Motel, the Lovers Swamp and Romp. The other motels are all too expensive. This one is free, but not free of eyes. It's the open air, nature all around you. The cars park over there and the couples walk to the edge of the river, make their way into the swamp. At low tide there's plenty of room but you have to be careful. There are lots of roots and holes. The rats don't usually bite, but it isn't a good idea to step on them either. Brecheiros—they're the ones who come to watch. They are the sort of men who can only realize their sexual fantasies by watching the couples in the Motel Manguezal. I've seen bullets flying in there. Some of the brecheiros get too close. But what they say is, "If you wanted privacy, you would go to a motel, instead of doing it here in public. Why are you here at the edge of the river in this place that's full of transvestites, gays, and lesbians, in the center of the city? You don't want privacy, you want to be observed."

**THE CHILDREN.** If you walk along any street, you're sure to cross paths with some who will accuse you for spare change. Or else they're on the bus and in a yawned monotone peddling candy or handkerchiefs or pencils. Their hair may be only half grown in, their bellies bloated or gaunt. There may even be something indifferent about the way the nine-year-old tells you how his mother beats him. Children of women who polish as they walk across floors that will never be their own, of ragpickers, of mothers who pray to God and all the spirits that they will never again spread their legs in labor but who still give birth three or four or five times more. Children who are neither a remedy for the past nor the hint of something better to come, only the luxuriance of the moment: castaways swimming for a receding shore, struggling the length of an impossible offing, but children all the same, with a glint of mischief, a breath of life.

*Um sopro de vida*, A Breath of Life, Clarice Lispector's posthumous novel pieced together from fragments the author left behind. The book's narrator, a writer, creates a character who in turn recreates the author. Zoë's was to have been a book about Aparecida, an ethnographic biography, yet oxymorons, like incompatible molecules, have a way of dissociating. The character is rewriting the author. Aparecida has turned her on her head, foiled the anthropologist's hope of suggesting a new form of collaboration in fieldwork. Aparecida is becoming the researcher. Recently she suggested they begin taking photographs of prostitutes at night, secretly, "like paparazzi. From a long way away, with a powerful lens."

Today they meet at the Law Faculty. Less private, but a respite from the smell off the river. Zoë arrives first and takes a seat on one of the ornate benches. The other benches are all occupied, some gardeners are digging up a bed of wilted flowers, and everywhere, just beyond the iron fence, the rumble of civilization.

"Would you like your shoes shined?" This is what the boy with the box slung over his shoulder asks. Is he too high to notice that Zoë is wearing sandals?

"No, thank you," she says.

A stupor, but on second thought not the sort induced by drugs. He is dumb with hunger, with parasites, with precocious resignation. He ambles toward the next potential client, the box heavy on his shoulder. Zoë calls out to him, gestures for him to come back. She offers the banana and the container of yoghurt she had brought for Aparecida. The boy is indifferent to the gesture but sits next to her, sucks the yoghurt out of the container and bites off pieces of the banana until there is nothing left but the skin, which he twirls around one finger.

He looks up, "You aren't from here, are you?"

"No. I am visiting. I am staying for a while." She doesn't want to talk about her life so she says, "How is business?"

"Some days I earn five reais, sometimes ten. Other days I come up with nothing. On those days I don't go home. Sometimes I stay out for three days, four days, then I go back. When I have some money for my family, I go home. It's like that. I get some money, I go home. If I have nothing, I wait a while, until I have something. If I have nothing, my brothers don't eat."

Zoë tries to think of something to say. In vain.

"Is it good there?" the boy asks.

"Where I am from?"

"Yes."

She thinks for a while. "Yes, it is good there. But children are not as good to their parents as you are to yours."

He has a mistrusting expression inside his mustache of yoghurt.

"A boy your age would not be feeding his little brothers and sisters."

"Who feeds them?"

"Their parents."

"The parents have money and the children eat what their parents give them?"

"Yes."

"Do you have some change for me, just a little."

She gives him a real, then another.

"*Fique com Deus* . . . Stay with God," he says, leaving Zoë to wonder why God is not with him.

"*Oi, Zoë,*" she calls out from the other side of the fence. Aparecida is wearing a crocheted top from which an asymmetrically stuffed bra protrudes and above which a tattoo is partially revealed. Until this time, Zoë had always seen her wearing something more discreet. The bra and its filling are new. Is her improved standard of living, now that I am paying her for interviews, making it possible for her to see an alternative to prostitution or is it merely deepening her relationship with the street? Zoë wonders.

"*Oi, Zoë, procurei você por tudo que é lugar* . . . I was looking for you everywhere."

Zoë doesn't reply to the untruth.

The gardeners look up at them for a long time.

Zoë gives her a set of three bottles of nail polish and a copy of *Marie Claire*. Aparecida examines the nail polish and then picks up the magazine and begins to leaf through the pages. She loves women's magazines. It is the pictures that capture her attention: advertisements for make-up, soap, jewelry, lingerie.

"Were you able to do any interviews?"

"Yes," she says, without looking up.

"Can we listen to them?"

"All right."

Aparecida presses the play button. There is a lot of white noise on the tape, or what Zoë thinks is white noise. Wind? Breathing? A muffled conversation in the background. Aparecida turns the page and looks at an advertisement for eye shadow. Every imaginable hue from peach to lime green.

"What is this?"

"Eye shadow."

"I mean on the tape."

"An encounter, last night."

"With whom?"

"Last night I was out on Mário Melo, walking around, looking at the city when a man came up to me." (Her professional encounters are always like that: she happens to be in a certain place, a man happens to approach her. The men are faceless.) "He said, 'Someone wants to talk to you.'" It was Flávia, a transvestite who is new to Mário Melo, who was looking for me. "She said, '*Ô, Aparecida*, this man wants a *suruba a três* . . . a ménage à trois. What do you think?' I didn't have any money and I was hungry so I said all right. The man said he would pay me ten and pay Flávia fifteen. I said I wanted fifteen too but Flávia said she was the one who had found the man. The man said that he was going to pay us twenty-five because that was all that he had. We could divide it up however we wanted. Since he didn't have any money for a motel, we went down to the edge of the river. I had the tape recorder in my bag and I turned it on."

There is an old lady on the next bench. She is turning in their direction. Zoë wants to lower the volume so the lady will not hear but also to raise it to know if she is actually hearing what Aparecida claims is on the tape. She raises it. The old lady scoots slightly toward the end of her bench, nearer them.

"You taped a session with a client?"

"I had the machine in my bag. This is the sort of thing you want to know about, isn't it?"

The man on the tape is muttering a plea.

"He wanted to have sex without a condom," Aparecida explains. "So I said, 'If you are going to penetrate me, put this on.'"

"You taped this?"

"Yes."

"Did he know you were taping him?"

"Of course not."

Aparecida proceeds to mouth the words in the advertisement for eye shadow.

"You didn't ask for permission?"

"No." She looks up, suddenly impatient. "I wanted it to be very spontaneous. Isn't that what you want? He was penetrating me, Flávia was licking him from behind. He didn't want to wear a condom but Flávia put it on for him."

Zoë feels a certain pain she cannot describe. The pain is not in her body.

"That's dangerous, you can't do that."

"I know. I never have sex without a condom."

"I mean you can't just record people without telling them."

"Who would guess they were being taped at a time like that?"

"If he had found out, he might have hurt you."

"He didn't find out."

"All right, he didn't. But he could have. Besides, you didn't have his permission. It isn't right."

"Did I give permission to the men who took me inside their cars when I was a child?"

Zoë says nothing.

At home, she doesn't throw away the tape, but she cannot bring herself to listen to it either.

When it was about four o'clock in the morning, a police van drove past. I was with Cibele and Grace. The police were looking for a transvestite who works on the Avenida Imbiribeira and who had robbed a client. So they stopped and made us line up and displayed us in front of the client, who was inside the car, to see if it had been one of us who had robbed him. He looked at each one of us, but he just said, "It wasn't that one, or that one, or that other one . . ." Still, the police put us inside a van. They asked for our papers. Some of us had documents, some of us didn't. When it was my turn to be asked, the policeman said, "Skinny faggot, let's see your papers." I told him I didn't have any. He hit me in the chest.

I said, "Hitting me in the chest isn't going to make them appear. They were lost in a fire."

He hit me in the shoulder.

At the station, I was locked in a cell with the other transvestites. When the station chief arrived, I discovered that he knew my grandfather. My grandfather, when he was alive, worked at a funeral home, and the station manager had gone there once, when his mother-in-law died. He transferred me to another cell, where I was alone. Even so, he kept me locked up there for three days.

When it was Saturday morning, I was given some cookies and a soft drink in a big two-liter bottle.

I didn't want to eat everything on my own, so I asked a policeman if he could let me out so I could share the food with my friends. The station manager had left for the day.

"All right," he said. "But you'll have to wash the two bathrooms and clean the fan, which is full of dust." He told me I had better not try to run away, because my situation could get a lot worse.

A prostitute arrived, a woman. The men made her take off her clothing.

When she was naked, she had some wounds on her body. And they said, "Woman, how much do you charge for a trick?"

"I charge thirty."

"Where would you find a man willing to pay thirty reais for what's left of your body?"

"I do this because I have four children to raise and their father is a useless leech," she said.

**THERE HAS BEEN A SPATE OF MURDERS.** Transvestites, reports
the *Folha de Pernambuco*, have been the target of unexplained violence. The *Folha* is the paper taxi drivers pick up to scan the photos
of corpses. The portrait of a bloodied body, a caption drawing attention to the mutilated genitalia. The transvestites themselves say
that the ones who are being murdered are the ones who like to rob
clients. But is there not more to this story? Why the magnitude of
the retaliation, why the sexual dismemberment?

And then, where else in the world do people receive infirm
strangers in their homes, bathe street children, share a cigarette
with the ragpicker? The extremes of cruelty and generosity, the
range of human possibilities are nowhere closer to the surface than
here. A federal deputy from the state of Acre, Zoë reads in the newspaper, is accused of an act of *falta de decoro parlamentar*, lack of
parliamentary decorum. His offense? Dismembering several of his
enemies with a chainsaw. Meanwhile, a beggar Zoë knows, who
plies the worshippers at São Bento, adopts an infant. Zoë asks her
why. "I felt sorry for him." His biological mother was a drug addict
and had the habit of extinguishing cigarettes on his skin. Cruelty is
at every social level but kindness is most readily found below a certain station. Now Zoë's neighbors are locked in debate over whether
the use of tinted windows should be allowed. The meeting takes
place one night in the building's *salão de festas*, or party room, on
the top floor. A number of people fear that smoked windows and
unattractive curtains could depress the value of the apartments in
the building.

Did you report the man?

At the hospital, when I arrived, the police asked me what had happened. I told them that a man had stabbed me. One of the men asked me where I had been stabbed. I showed the wound in my stomach. The same man said, "So the fellow was only trying to do you a favor. He wanted to give you a cunt."

**APARECIDA LEADS HER** through the entry to the blue-green building, into an area where parties are held. "This is where they serve the food," she says, pointing to a counter. It is empty today. The simple red tiles on the roof are supported by wooden beams. Zoë and Aparecida walk out into a courtyard, a small area of green amid the neighboring apartment buildings.

"This is where I would sleep," Aparecida says. They enter. A single long urinal lines one wall, the rusting metal frames of chairs someone decided to store are littered about the floor. It was once a men's bathroom.

Lena's compound, as it were. Her father is the caretaker for the Clube América, which is rented to soccer teams, companies, and families bristling with children, uncles, aunts, and cousins. A place for parties. Lena's father is expected to live on the premises and, with consent or not, he has built another small house for Lena. The breezeblock walls of her house are intact but the roof is apt to leak when the wind and rain are very strong.

Aparecida claps outside the door and in a minute or two a young man, Lena's nephew, appears—not from inside but from behind. Lena is not home yet. The nephew shows no sign of being surprised or happy to see Aparecida. He opens up and then returns to his grandfather's house next door. Within moments, Aparecida, who has taken a seat on the sofa, her head slouched back and mouth open, is asleep.

A naked bulb lights the living room, which is also the site of the kitchen because there is an old gas stove and a basin to one side.

A long time goes by. Zoë reaches for a yellowing newspaper on the table and reads about a famine in North Korea. The article is accompanied by a photograph of a toddler with protruding bones and on one of whose glassy eyes a fly is perched, or perhaps walking. You can't tell because the photograph was taken in something like one two hundred and fiftieth of a second and at that speed even the movements of flies are difficult to capture. Outside the realm of the photograph, one can only assume that the child is now dead and buried; only his look of frozen resignation remains.

"The famine is always somewhere else," Zoë scribbles in her notebook. The first time she was here, the famine was in Sudan. Middle-class women at an Olinda church had held a bake sale for the victims on a continent they would never visit and then went on paying their maids salaries that allowed for the purchase of little more than rice and beans.

When Lena arrives it is dark and Zoë is almost asleep.

"*Bicha maluca*," Lena cries out. Aparecida stands and hugs her and shows no signs of having been asleep. "*Pensei que tu não ia voltar mais . . .* I thought you would never come back."

"I'll always come back to see you. *Imagina!* How could you say that? This is Zoë."

Zoë reaches out to shake the hand of a woman of her own age but with the full weight of having become a mother when her breasts were barely raised. There is no place in the world where children are more beautiful or where beauty fades faster. As a child Lena must have been beautiful, Zoë thinks to herself.

"Would you like some water?"

Zoë accepts, but when she has the glass in hand, she is afraid to drink from it. Was the little jar in the refrigerator drawn straight from the tap? When Zoë brings the glass to her lips, she doesn't quite drink. Aparecida drinks hers in one gulp and asks for another.

"Where have you been? I looked for you everywhere."

"I was in the city."

"*Estava doida pra te ver . . .* I was dying to see you. I looked for you in Rio Branco, all over the city . . ."

"These are for you," Aparecida cuts her off, handing Lena one gift after another: a pair of green stretch pants and a matching top, a diadem, a bottle of nail polish (from the set of three that Zoë had given her), face powder, a bottle of perfume. It seems to Zoë that nearly all the money she had given Aparecida the day before was spent on these presents. Or perhaps all and then some.

Lena reproaches her for the largesse but joyfully examines the gifts. What would Malinowski, the father of anthropology as a science, say about this? What obligations are being forged? Or is Aparecida giving these things selflessly? The functionalists never contemplated that possibility. Are all human acts the result of a spoken or unspoken calculation?

"This is Zoë," Aparecida repeats. "She is writing a book about me and would like to interview you."

"I wanted to meet you . . ." Zoë says, shifting her weight uncomfortably.

"Aparecida told me about you when he called." Lena speaks of Aparecida as a man.

"Get the tape recorder," Aparecida orders.

"I don't think that is necessary."

"It's all right," Lena says. "You can interview me. Aparecida has told me about the book you are writing."

"She wants to be in it, "Aparecida says.

"I am just trying to learn about Aparecida's life. I don't know if what we are writing will become a book . . ."

"Lena, your testimony is going to be essential," Aparecida interrupts in a professional tone.

Sifting through Zoë's bag, Aparecida finds the tape recorder and conducts the interview herself. She inquires about herself in the third person: What made you decide to help Aparecida? Where did you meet Aparecida? What did you think about the fact that Aparecida is a transvestite? What do other people think about Aparecida?

Aparecida, as Zoë learns, was sitting on the street outside the club one day and as Lena walked out of the compound Aparecida asked her for some water.

"I said, 'What are you doing sitting in the street like this?' He told me he lived in the street. I went inside and got him some water and also a plate of food. I felt sorry for him. The next day he was there again, sniffing from a bottle of glue. I went inside, got some food and water and came back out again and said, 'Why are you out here? Don't you have a place to live?' That was when he told me about what had happened to him at home and why he lived in the street.

"After a while, when I saw him almost every day, I told him to come inside. He came inside but he only wanted to come in as far as this area." Lena points toward what used to be the men's bathroom. "I told him that only dogs sleep outside of houses and that he should stay in my house, in the living room, but he didn't want to. He would stay out there and sniff glue and disappear at night to walk the streets. But we became friends and I told him he had no need to do that. I told him, 'If you don't have a job, I can feed you. You can sleep here and I'll give you food,' because I don't like to see anyone go hungry. My mother was from the *interior* and sometimes when we were little she would take us there, so I saw people who were hungry. A lot of people around here are hungry too, so I know what it is to want to eat and have nothing.

"I have a daughter, but she got together with a man and even though they don't have any children yet, they live together. My father lives next door, but I'm alone here. That's why I would like Aparecida to live here with me."

"If you were president of the country, what would you do for street children?" Aparecida says, trying to change the subject.

"You would like Aparecida to live with you?" Zoë asks. She feels the sort of happiness that comes only in combination with disbelief.

"The doors of my house are always open for him. He can even sleep in my bed. The minute and hour he wants to come here, he can come."

"*Lena, você é ótima!* . . . Lena, you are divine," says Aparecida, and turning toward Zoë: "She accepts me the way I am, like a mother. Lena is almost like a mother to me. Like a sister and like a mother. Lena, during the time you have known Aparecida . . ."

"You would like her to stay with you?" Zoë repeats.

"Yes. The minute and hour he wants to come here, he can come. That's what I said. When he was here before, he would stay out there. I think it would be better if he stayed inside."

"Lena, do you think that the death penalty should be applied to people who sexually exploit children?" Aparecida interjects.

"So you would like her to stay with you now?" Zoë asks.

"Yes."

"That wouldn't work," Aparecida decrees, reluctantly coming back to the topic of conversation at hand. "I'm too busy now with the work I'm doing with Zoë. It's a book about my life in the street. I have to be in the street, in the center of the city."

"You've lived in the street long enough to write several books," Zoë tells her. "Where you live now has nothing to do with our work."

With the beginnings of a knowing smile on her lips, Lena says nothing.

"It might be a good idea later, but not now. Maybe in a few months. In a few months it would be good," Aparecida replies.

Zoë refuses to believe what she is hearing. There must be a misunderstanding. "Aparecida, I don't think you understand. Lena is saying that she would like you to live in her house."

"Yes, Lena is divine. When I get ready to go to sleep at night, I say a prayer for Lena. Every night. I get ready to sleep and I pray for her. The same way I pray for my mother and for my brothers and sisters."

"You can have a place to stay," Zoë tells her.

"I would like to stay with Lena, but just now I need to resolve some other problems. My things are scattered around in different people's houses. I need to collect my belongings and that will take a while . . . Zoë, when you were in the bathroom, Lena mentioned to me that she needs to buy some medicine and that she doesn't have the money for it now. Could you give her ten reais? I'll pay you back."

"Yes, if you will agree to live with Lena."

No one says anything.

As they are leaving, walking toward the bus stop, Aparecida asks for another ten reais, this time for herself.

"I won't give you another cent unless you move in with Lena," Zoë tells her.

"You are very difficult to understand," Aparecida replies.

"Is it me we are trying to understand?"

"What good would it do for me to tell you that I am going to get my things and come back right away? You don't want me to lie to you, do you?"

"But why would it have to be a lie?"

"You are only seeing one side of Lena. You come here for a little while and you think you understand everything."

"I understand that Lena is a good woman."

"Lena is divine."

"So what is the problem?"

"Lena is divine, but I am not welcome there."

"It's her house. She wants you there."

"She says she wants me to stay, but I don't know that. How do you know what another person wants? You are only hearing what other people are saying and you are seeing what they are doing, but you are not hearing or seeing what they are thinking. Lena says she wants me here, but her brother comes to the house and says that Lena can't have a person from the street living there, that I am going to steal her things. If it is her house, she has to tell him that he cannot say those things, but she doesn't . . ."

"You have been blackmailing me."

"*O quê!*"

"You tell me that you have no money, that you have no place to go, that you will have to go out onto the avenue because you have no money. You say that because you know I don't want to see you on the avenue. You say it so I will give you money. And then you go out and do what you are going to do."

"So I am an actress?"

Zoë doesn't have a reply.

"You think I go out on the avenue and wait for men to come and tell me to get inside their cars because I like it. That I risk my life for the fun of it?"

"All I know is that you don't have to do it. You could live with Lena. I can try to sell your paintings. We can try to find you a job."

"I would like to have a house and a job but I don't. I would like to have a refrigerator full of food, but I don't. Not everything is the way we would like it to be. And when we have the chance, we don't do everything we want to do. When I was Beto, why did you invite me into your house? Why did you feed me things I had never eaten before and would never taste again? Why did you wash my hair and dress me in new clothing? Was it to help me or to fix something inside you?"

At the bus stop they part in silence.

**HOW DO WE KNOW** what anyone else is thinking? Zoë wonders. She does not have an answer. She was trained only to observe, to listen. She does both of those things. From one window, Zoë can see the same woman passing by each day and inspecting the trash left outside the building. Through another window, in New York, she once saw a teenage boy in a neighboring apartment. A gust of wind and for a brief moment the curtain reveals the boy naked, watching himself in the mirror, his hand twitching between his legs. But who is to say what makes him do those things, what image was in his mind? Is it possible to know what the woman thinks when she finds the half-chewed drumstick? Does she conjure up the face of the girl who chewed the other half? A penis in a slippery hand, decaying food. These are the things we see. But do we know what is behind them?

I have no idea what Aparecida thinks, Zoë admits to herself.

But this is what I think she thinks, she continues: I am a client. Is she not in the business of selling fantasies, of satisfying fantasies? "They come to me to realize the fantasies they cannot realize at home, with their wives." This is how she describes it. "I give them something they do not have."

Aparecida guesses what the client cannot do at home, in the home where he raises two children and gives his wife the money to re-upholster the sofa, where sex is in the missionary position and the house is painted in time for New Year's. The street, the home, the favorite prism of Brazilian sociologists, the inventive possibilities of the nocturnal confusion between the big house and the slave quarters; but what of the moment where the man of the modern apartment building meets the transvestite on the avenue? Children cannot be born of that encounter, but something else surely is. It is a game of guessing. What is the man seeking? As in any game of guessing, Aparecida cannot be certain; so she gives the client what she thinks he wants. Does this one want a virile woman or a demure, unassuming man with a hint of breasts? Does he want her to ask whether next time he might not sneak her a pair of his wife's panties? Even if there is not a next time, is the question not a part of the fantasy the client wants to fulfill? The demiwoman dressed as demiwife. If he says he wants to use Aparecida as a woman, why has he not, then, sought a woman, a woman made by God? Mechanics or transgression, which is he after?

So she has tried to guess my fantasy, Zoë thinks. Or rather my fantasies, because when Aparecida was Beto, I had another fantasy. But in a sense, she corrects herself, they are the same: to save Aparecida from the life she is leading. That is what she thinks Aparecida thinks. For street children, of whom Aparecida was once one, the street is that place outside the home: buildings and houses seen from the exterior. But it is not simply a physical place, a site captured through the camera lens, by the gaze of the driver as he makes his way across the city. A lot of people can be found *in* the street, but change the preposition and we see that it makes a world of difference: *on* the street is not the same thing. Superimposed on that physical space is that life, *essa vida*; that is what the children call the street. It is the life they lead there, stealing, sniffing glue, selling their bodies. That is the life they have *fallen into*.

*Eu caí nessa vida aos nove anos de idade* . . . I landed in this life when I was eight years old. Aparecida landed in—"fell into"—that life and has not pulled herself out. Her contemporaries are mostly dead. She is a walking reminder that fathers rape. My first fantasy was to be her mother, Zoë thinks, but a mother who hid behind the reality that she wasn't a mother. Like the client who sought one thing at home and another in the street, I could be one thing to Beto and another to the neighbors. A fantasy that could be hidden, precisely because it did not require every implication of enactment. And now I have traveled from *lá*, or there, and taken it upon myself to awaken in her the desire to overcome her trauma, to lead another life. And so it is that she tells me that since we met, she has given up sniffing glue. She has begun to give value to her life. And yet, the smell of alcohol on her breath, the bottle of glue in her purse?

The fantasy having been identified, Aparecida's job, it seems to Zoë, is to make it come true—in the realm of fantasy. She now wants to pull herself out of that life. That is what she thinks I want for her: a home, a job, a refrigerator full of food. I want to awaken that desire in her so that she will give up the life she is leading in the street. This client is after nothing less than birth—rebirth. So we are engaged in an act of procreation, after all, Zoë concludes. The two of us wombless but together aiming to give birth. The two of us, after life.

If she declines the possibility to live in the house of a woman who loves her and who will feed her and protect her, does it mean that the life she leads in the street is the one she wants? Does she really seek to stop sniffing glue, selling her body, sleeping in the street? Has it occurred to her, Zoë asks herself, that I might have considered that this is the life she intends to continue leading?

Of course not. Otherwise she would have given up the game for lost long ago.

**THE NEXT WEEK**, Aparecida is nowhere to be found.

Perhaps her economy is not as simple as second-guessing the fantasies of strangers, storing wealth by giving gifts. There is a moral plane that has nothing to do with exchange theory, ancient or postmodern: the moral plane of lightness. She can live light not merely because all her possessions could fit inside a few shopping bags but because she can wake and sleep when she wants, seek food when she is hungry, move on when she has had enough. A hunter and gatherer? No, she herself is hunted, she is eaten. A case of the prey that seeks the raptor? But when it comes to the nuisance that is authority, any that impinges on her, this is a passing problem. As with the nomad, conflict is resolved by roaming: the plains are vast, the river has two sides—maybe three—the streets are labyrinthine.

Several nights in a row Zoë goes to the Rua da Aurora. One night Cleópatra Honey is standing in the semidarkness of the corner of Mário Melo and the Rua da Fundição, behind her the wall enclosing the parking lot where the sex workers sometimes take their clients. She doesn't much want to talk but goes as far as saying she hasn't seen Aparecida *faz um tempão*, for the longest time, as it were.

Flávia is less ill disposed but she likewise reveals nothing about Aparecida's whereabouts. "She's probably out on Imbiribeira."

Zoë asks Dona Marisa, who sells cake and hotdogs on the corner of Mário Melo and Cruz Cabugá, to accept a note for Aparecida and to give it to her if she comes by.

**AN ARGUMENT WITH FÁTIMA.** There are different sorts of needs, she tells Zoë. One variety she identifies as felt needs, the other as real needs. If you go into a community and ask the people what they need, they will tell you a soccer field. That's what they feel they need. But if you engage them in a process of reflection about their lives, they will see that what they really need is to vaccinate their children, cover up the open sewerage lines, reduce the incidence of domestic violence. As an educator, *um educador*, someone working in the tradition of Paulo Freire's pedagogy of the oppressed, one's job is to help people distinguish between one sort of need and another.

If this is the lens through which Aparecida's life can be apprehended, what are her needs, real and felt? Is it not true that she *needs* to live in a house? Since she will not live with Lena, should I buy her a house? Zoë wonders. What is the sense of studying a life in the street when what I should be trying to do is make certain that this life, Aparecida's, not be led in the street?

Another afternoon and Aparecida is still nowhere to be found. Dust rides the shafts of waning sunlight. Zoë approaches the Torture Never Again monument. It is four o'clock, and the park is mostly abandoned. The tide is high so she sits facing the swollen river and tries to make out the nature of the sunken objects: tatters of plastic bags, bottles of bleach, candy wrappers. The lives of dispossessed objects. On the ground, a big leaf flutters but when Zoë puts on her glasses to have a closer look, it is a rat.

*Without those things, where would we be? The dogs, the cats, the night, the rats that sometimes crawl onto the cardboard where we lay our heads . . .*

The solitude is broken by a group of youths, one of whom motions toward Zoë. They are approaching, several of them holding plastic bottles to their mouths: *os cheira-colas*, glue sniffers. At another moment Zoë's pulse might quicken and her breaths draw shallow. But she is unafraid. The five adolescent boys and one young girl with a stupefied gait come up to her. Extending one hand, the girl asks for some change. She is wearing a tank top and one shoulder is red with iodine: a wound someone treated. In her other hand she holds something wrapped in a dirty towel.

Zoë takes out a package of cookies from her bag. There is a smell of glue on the girl's breath. She grabs the whole roll. The boys grab too. The wrapper breaks and the cookies, twenty or thirty of them, scatter across the ground. The boys are picking up as many as they can, with no regard for how many the others have collected. When there are no more cookies on the ground, only a moment or two later, one boy says something Zoë doesn't understand but it makes the others laugh. Only small crumbs are left behind when the group staggers off. They have eaten something and now they are holding the bottles to their mouths again. Suddenly the girl turns back, as if she had forgotten something. Her hair is sun-bleached against her dark skin. Her breasts are large beneath the T-shirt. She walks up to Zoë. The others continue on as if the girl had never been part of the group.

"Tia," she says, "*segura aí . . .* hold this, lady . . . *Demoro não . . .* I won't be long." She doesn't wait for a reply before stooping to lower the towel and its contents into Zoë's lap. Zoë's gaze is fixed on the girl but her hands tell her what she is holding. She wants to protest but when she opens her mouth there are no words to express her astonishment. The girl ambles away. Only when she has disappeared behind the trees does Zoë lower her gaze toward the warmth in her lap that she knows is a baby.

A part of her wants to stand and run after the mother, another simply disbelieves. So she cradles the child in silence until she decides to slowly pull back the towel. The front half of the infant's head is bare. Elsewhere the hair grows only sparsely. The tiny ears are pierced, and there is something disconcerting about the child's shallow breaths.

The towel smells of urine, and worse. Zoë lifts the baby away from the soiled cloth. The infant, otherwise naked, is wearing a T-shirt with the peeling, misspelled words Happy-Go-Lacky embossed on the front. On the plane they had given Zoë a cloth in a small sealed package, to clean her face or her hands, which she had kept with her in her bag. She begins to swab the baby, who remains expressionless. She lifts the shirt and wipes the child's torso, revealing the insect bites that are swollen with scratching. The shirt is caked with dried feces. Zoë's hands become soiled, and the towelette is now dirty as well. There is a spigot nearby and she takes the shirt to rinse it but the rusty handle won't turn.

It is only the two of them now, Zoë and the infant. The girl caught up with her companions and all of them have disappeared across the avenue and down a side street. This baby doesn't see me with her eyes, Zoë thinks to herself. She looks past me, through me, around me, as if for her looking and perceiving were discrete acts.

Where is the place for grief—imported for what it's worth—in a land where someone is always upturning the last stone in search of something to eat, where an overpass can be a roof, where entire families live in shacks no larger than a bathroom, where a mother, herself a girl, leaves a baby in a stranger's lap: casually, as one might ask someone to hold one's place in the checkout line at the grocery store? I've forgotten the eggs, do you mind . . . ? I'll be right back.

And the recollection, Aparecida's caveat: *"There is no such thing as children of the street. No one is born to grow up in the street. We just fall here."*

A baby has fallen into my lap, the realization quickens.

A smell wafting off the river, the sun moving west. No one notices Zoë, or the baby. What would be unusual? A mother with her infant child in the park.

A young couple strolls past, slowly, holding hands. He is touching the back of the girl's neck. She wears a blue dress that quivers slightly in the wind.

The baby isn't stirring. The mother is nowhere to be seen. Time is different here. What does it mean, "I won't be long?" Her own grandmother may have used those words when she left Salonika. The shafts of sunlight, the dust, the smells off the river, the rats. Have the fish consumed my mother's ashes?

And if I stood?

And if I . . . ?

A bubble has formed on the infant's lips, round and tiny and inscrutable like a planet seen from a great distance. The couple has taken a seat on a bench. Her head is nestled in the crook of his neck.

*. . . If you ask me, we know only the afternoon, where we are today, but no one knows what will happen when night falls. At any moment we can be set alight; there are people who would do that: throw gasoline on us, toss a match. That is the risk we run. But life is the trees, the birds, all the things of nature taken together. Without those things, where would we be? The dogs, the cats, the night, the rats that sometimes crawl onto the cardboard where we lay our heads. All of that is a form of life . . .*

The baby isn't stirring, but for a moment she seems to be looking at Zoë, not through her. Her eyes are a deep brown under a watery film that can't possibly protect her from the cruelty she will witness in life. Zoë could get up now, she could walk away with the warmth she holds in her arms. The shafts of light are becoming fewer and fainter and more difficult to distinguish from dusk.

Clutching her with a force of concentration that verges on awkwardness, Zoë rocks the baby slightly and strokes her back. Had her own mother done that with her? How is it that the deepest love many of us ever receive in life is utterly forgotten? *Amor só de mãe . . .* If I were to give her a name, I know what that would be, Zoë thinks to herself. Jews and their circularity, secreting the dead back into the present through the least suspecting, those too young to protest.

With her tiny fingers, the baby is reaching toward the open length between two buttons on Zoë's shirt. For a hand that size, it wouldn't seem to be a difficult target, but the hand and the desire that move it understand one another poorly. The baby issues a muted pout after the first unsuccessful attempt, before trying again. The effort tires her, perhaps the frustration as well. As suddenly as she had decided to reach for Zoë's breast, the baby closes her eyes and seems to be asleep or prepared for sleep. She has used her last reserves in an effort to satisfy an urge. Dusk is falling, the baby is breathing its shallow breaths, the park is almost empty now. If she sits right there, with time Zoë might sense the approach of steps, notice the scent of glue, and hear the only words that fit this picture: "*Obrigada* . . . Thank you. In this life, my daughter is all I have."

## Acknowledgments

My thanks go first to Bruna Veríssimo, for her art of conversation, her patience, her quiet contemplation of what is important in life, and her penchant for finding moments of joy, despite all odds.

The H. F. Guggenheim Foundation supported this project—"as an experiment," in the words of one representative; I am very grateful that they took the risk and hope not to have let them down.

Keith Hart has been my mentor in anthropology and writing for more than a decade. He helped me with this work from long before I knew what it would be about.

Roshila Nair, Zildo Rocha, Enrico Mario Santí, Paula Fass, and João Biehl all offered valuable criticism on parts of the book or the work as a whole.

And my thanks to Isabel Balseiro for all that life.

## A Note on the Photographs

All children who appear in photographs in this book are adults today, if they are alive. In accordance with Brazilian law, and common sense, no images that could endanger living children have been included.

## Illustration Credits

Daniel Aamot: 47, 53, 85
Isabel Balseiro: 42, 69, 71, 79, 106, 140, 157, 174
Tobias Hecht: 20
Sourena Mohammadi: 3, 19, 29, 96

Woodcut, detail from "Cutting Up the Corpse." Theodor De Bry, *America*, part 3, *Accounts from the Brazilian Provinces*; after Hans Staden (c. 1525–1575), *True History and Description of a Land of Savages* (Marburg, 1557; reprint, Frankfurt, 1592): 121.

**Tobias Hecht's** first book, *At Home in the Street: Street Children of Northeast Brazil*, won the 2002 Margaret Mead award. His subsequent books include *Minor Omissions: Children in Latin American History and Society* (editor) and *The Museum of Useless Efforts* (translator). He has won writing and research awards from the H. F. Guggenheim Foundation and the National Endowment for the Humanities, and his short story "La ventana" was a finalist for the 2004 Hucha de Oro, considered Spain's most important literary prize in the category of the short story. This is his first novel.

**Bruna Veríssimo** (a pseudonym), whose spoken and written narratives inspired portions of this novel, was born in Recife, Brazil, in 1975. With no formal schooling, she left home at the age of eight and has lived in the street almost continuously since then. She taught herself to read and write as well as to paint, crochet, and design clothing. A member of Brazil's National Movement of Street Children as an adolescent, she has been a sex worker from the age of seven.

*Library of Congress Cataloging-in-Publication Data*

Hecht, Tobias, 1964-

After life : an ethnographic novel / Tobias Hecht ; with
portions based on the narrations of Bruna Veríssimo.

p. cm.

Includes bibliographical references.

ISBN 0-8223-3750-9 (alk. paper)

ISBN 0-8223-3788-6 (pbk. : alk. paper)

I. Title.

PS3608.E287A69 2006

813'.6—dc22     2005028240